Be Still My

Bleating Heart

Hannah Reed

And come he slow, or come he fast, it is but death who comes at last ~ Sir Walter Scott

Chapter 1

Squirreled away in my favorite corner of the Kilt & Thistle Pub, I was vaguely aware of the hum of conversation in the background, reminding me of the soothing warm vibrations flowing from a Scottish harp. Usually, the pub brings forth my creative juices and, as a romance author, contracted and with deadlines to meet, this place has been as important to me as the setting of my stories is to my readers. However, the blank laptop screen in front of me was a serious indication that a cloud of dreaded writer's block had descended. It had happened as quickly as fog on a Highland moor.

Home these days is a cottage on a working sheep farm, where I happily retreat whenever possible. During the day, a tucked-away table at the

Kilt & Thistle serves quite nicely for my current work-in-progress. Before arriving in Glenkillen, I was an orphan, adrift and lonely, if one can still be called a waif at thirty-eight years old. Sadly, my mother and father are both gone and I have no siblings. Here in the Highlands, I've finally found my place with close friends, distant family members on my paternal side, and work I love.

So why the block?

I had my suspicions. Perhaps a symptom of my lack-luster personal life with the consequences being nothing exciting to transpose to the written page. Or maybe I simply needed a break from writing. I'd finished and submitted two books in the Highland Love Series back-to-back and needed to turn in book number three by the end of the year. A few weeks off during the flowering month of May might do me some good.

As I pondered the dilemma, a text message, announced by a piano riff, came in from my stateside best friend. Ami Pederson, bestselling historical romance author, pounding out one best seller after another. She's happily married, wealthy, and extremely pushy in a loving sort of way. Ami was the reason for my arrival in Scotland.

"Any hot new sex scenes smoking up your story, soon-to-be famous Eden Elliott?" she queried.

I couldn't lie about the non-existent scenes because then she'd want to read them.

"Been busy on a case," I lied instead, referring to my unusual part-time position as a special constable, aka volunteer police officer. Yes, the position really exists in Scotland as well as in the whole of Great Britain. I serve at the pleasure of Inspector Jamieson, or rather, in spite of his displeasure. Although, lately he has been less prickly, a hopeful sign that he finds my assistance acceptable.

He'd been pressured from above to accept a special constable and, after barely arriving in Glenkillen, I happened to be standing over a dead body and seemed his best choice at the time. Regardless of the initial circumstances that brought me to his small investigative team and my ongoing first-timer jitters, the position gives me a nice balance, grounding me in the complexities of reality when I'm not writing romantic fiction.

"A very complex case," I texted to Ami, digging deeper into the deception. "I'll tell you about it later."

A text came back immediately. "How about your own love life? Have you consummated with that lovely Scot yet?"

I groaned. Once Ami locks onto an idea, she can't let it go. Leith Cameron is a good-looking man. His exceptional attributes figure prominently in the romantic love interests I create. And he's kind and thoughtful, his inner beauty matching the outer.

But...see that was the thing. The big *BUT*. Leith has never given me so much as a hint that he's interested in romancing me. And I'd much rather have our friendly relationship than risk losing it by pushing for something more. If I can accept that, why can't Ami? Of course, she claims that I'm missing the signs, that he's signaling, and I'm too slow to pick them up. She'd say anything to further her match-making scheme.

One thing she might be right about, although I'll never admit it to her, is that my imagination seems to have run out of titillating love scenes. Ami has claimed in the past that I'll have to immerse myself in a romance at some point or the well will run dry. Had the well stopped flowing? Or did I simply have spring fever?

The days are longer now. Birds are singing and building nests. Clusters of bluebells, which are also known as Fairies' Thimbles, grow in vibrant violet-blue clusters on heathlands and verges. I'd walked among them recently. Locals might blame this block on me, claiming I'd displeased the fairies from the ancient legends.

I shook that ridiculous thought away, sighed, and slid the phone into my pocket without responding to Ami. Then I closed the laptop, concealing the wordless screen, and glanced up to see Bill Morris and his nephew, Andy, at a table nearby. I'd been so absorbed in thought that I hadn't even noticed them come in.

Not that their appearance was extraordinary. Bill is a common fixture at the pub. He owns The Whistling Inn next door, but as far as I can tell, he does nothing to keep it going, though he occupies one of the rooms on a permanent basis. The inn's success is due to his daughter, Jeannie. Andy was the latest relative to join the staff after his parents sent him from Oban to help out.

After careful observation, I've decided that there are pros and cons to living next door to a pub. Bill certainly doesn't have to go far at closing time and doesn't have to get behind the wheel of a car. On the other hand, he strolls over from the inn, starts drinking early, and usually passes out, at which point Jeannie, or now Andy, has to come and haul him away.

Bill had started on his first pint. Andy, although of legal drinking age, was responsibly nursing a bottle of Irn-Bru, the national soft drink – a sweet concoction, loaded with additives, and not a personal favorite of mine.

Andy seemed a bit surly, judging by the set of his jaw, his patchwork of freckles a bit more colorful than usual, probably not appreciating having to babysitting his uncle.

"One is the limit f...fer ye," I heard Andy say, with a hint of a stammer, which I had noticed when he'd first arrived. His stammer seemed to become more pronounced if he became excited. "And then it's b...back tae the inn tae help out."

"Says yerself?" Bill asked.

"Says Jeannie," Andy went on. "Ye been killing yerself slowly and it has tae stop, she says. I shouldn't o' let ye t...talk me intae even this one."

Bill snorted. "Try tae stop me, ye wee scarecrow."

If I had to pick sides in a wrestling match, I'd bet on Bill, who had at least a hundred pounds on his nephew. But before I could decide on a hefty monetary amount for my imaginary wager, Sean Stevens entered the pub and zeroed in on my table.

"I don't mean tae bother ye," he said, taking a seat across from me.

Interrupting was exactly his intention. Those more thoughtful give me a wide berth when I'm in writing mode, respecting my space. Not Sean. Or rather Police Officer Stevens, the newest addition to the force, who wore his uniform with brimming pride. Today his slight form sported the standard white shirt, black tie, and peaked cap of the local cops.

"Are you here on official business?" I asked, which is the only explanation I'd considered worthy of an intrusion by Sean. Granted, I'd been absorbed in pretty much everything except writing, but still.

"Nothin' such as that. I have some spare time. Besides, a wee burdie told me ye'd need company since Leith isn't around tae entertain ye."

His silly smirk reminded me that Sean was also in on the Leith-is-the-one-for-you conspiracy.

He continued, "Takin' care of business out on the sea in his fishing guide boat, he is. We won't see hide nor hair o' him for weeks. Any spare time he gets, will be taken up by that daughter of his."

Leith *does* keep busy. Arranging fishing expeditions on his boat named *Bragging Rights,* growing barley at his croft farm for distribution to the local distilleries, and co-raising his six-year-old daughter, Fia, from a failed relationship with the child's mother.

My mind wandered to a recurring dream I'd been having. In the dream, a man comes to me while I'm lying in a canopy bed covered with a soft white duvet. His face is hidden in shadow, the room semi-dark, but I sense that I know him intimately. He approaches my bed. I open my arms to him. He joins me, his strong hands caressing my body. We make love, first slowly and tenderly, then with growing passion.

I shook myself back to the present, letting the daydream drift away.

I wonder how Ami would interpret *that* sign?

"Is Vicki getting ready for tonight?" I asked, turning my attention to a safer subject.

Vicki MacBride was the first friend I made on arriving in the Highlands, and she owns the sheep farm where I live. Raised in California, but Scottish by birth, she inherited a beautiful property on the outskirts of Glenkillen. She's also engaged to Sean.

"Vicki's over at the bookshop," her fiancé said. "I'm driving her home in a bit. She's all excited about goin' tae that Scott Supper staged at the home of Derrick and Brenda Findlay. Ye know, all that *'O' what a tangled web we weave when first we practice to deceive.*"

I smiled. "Look at you, quoting Sir Walter Scott!"

"I'm more worldly than I appear on the surface," Sean said preening. "How about yerself? Lookin' forward to yer first Scott supper tonight?"

"I am, very much."

The Sir Walter Scott Club's next meeting was only a few hours away. According to Vicki, the suppers are glorious celebrations of the author's life and works. The prolific Scottish novelist, poet, playwright, and historian is highly honored throughout Scotland.

I imagined that the evening would most likely include traditional music, recitation of carefully selected passages, and a high consumption of whisky

11

along with Scottish dishes such as haggis, tatties, and neeps. For the uninitiated, that translates to animal offal, mashed potatoes, and rutabaga, all of which I sampled early on thanks to the Inspector. Jamieson had described haggis as sheep's pluck. Later, I would discover he was referring to internal organs. Not for everybody, although it goes down easiest with whisky.

"How's the writin' coming?" Sean wanted to know.

"It's not," I admitted. "I'm considering taking a break, or maybe writing something different than the series. Something that I can wrap up in a few weeks, a month at most. A short story maybe."

That had a certain appeal.

"Ye can write a true story about me," Sean suggested, not the first person to think his life was exciting enough for the written page. "I'm as interesting as ye get. Or…ye could make yerself useful and do a bit of legwork on the Pensioner Robber case."

"No leads yet?"

"Not a one."

The Pensioner Robber, as we've privately dubbed him, had struck three times in the last ten days, always in the same fashion, targeting female senior citizens inside their cars, holding them at knifepoint, and demanding their purses. So far, no one had been physically injured, but it was only a matter of time before something tragic occurred.

Sean shook his head, sadly. "Tis a despicable person who targets old persons."

I nodded my agreement then noticed my boss entering the pub behind several other patrons making their way to tables.

Detective Inspector Jamieson was a widower in his late fifties, tall, imposing, and intensely focused on the business of law enforcement. Today, he wore his standard uniform under a black Inverness dress coat; khakis, a blue button down with the top button open, and a loose tie His somber personality was the exact opposite of the easy-going, fun-loving Leith's.

Jamieson's piercing blue eyes found my table immediately.

"Constable Elliott," he curtly acknowledged my presence before turning his attention to Sean. "The robber has struck again. This time the victim was forced at knife-point into the boot. I need ye tae get out tae the edge o' Glenkillen and assess the scene and canvass fer witnesses."

Jamieson gave him the location.

"I'm ontae it." Sean jumped up, then paused. "I'm supposed tae collect Vicki from the bookshop."

"I'll get her," I offered. "You go on."

"I'll let her know about the change in plans." Sean hustled away, a fire lighting up his eyes.

"You have to admire his eagerness," I pointed out, aware of the inspector's opinion of Sean, which wasn't high. "Do you want me to go out there, too? I'd have to bring Vicki along, but she wouldn't mind."

The inspector took the seat that Sean had occupied. "Tis mostly handled. I came here from interviewing the poor woman. Chust thought I'd find something fer our Sean to help with tae keep him outta my hair. The sod took the woman's mobile and purse and locked her in the boot fer over an hour, according tae her."

"Is she okay?" I asked, noting with pleasure how easily I now understood his heavy Scottish accent compared to the day I'd first met him.

"Aye. She appears tae not be one tae go down easily. A passer-byer heard banging and released her. She came outta the boot ready fer a fight. Fer a pensioner, she sure has the spunk. Same description by this victim as the others gave. The bloke had a local accent, was average height and weight, and was wearing one o' those three-hole full-head black ski masks. Glenkillen is goin' tae get a reputation as a car robbery hotspot if we don't catch this Jimmy soon."

He noted my confusion. "Jimmy isn't his actual name," he explained. "'Tis an expression. Means guy, ye know, same as bloke."

Oh, ok.

While Jamieson took a call on his cell phone, I checked the time on my own phone. Just after three p.m. Assuming less than an hour had elapsed between the call to the police and the inspector's appearance at the pub, and allowing for the time the woman had been locked in the trunk, the robbery had occurred at approximately one o'clock. Give or take. The perpetrator had plenty of time to disappear, leaving no tracks. Why hadn't any witnesses come forward? This was number four. A man wearing a ski mask isn't exactly commonplace.

But the attacks had all been outside the village center. Fewer potential eyes to witness the crime.

Jamieson finished his conversation, tucked the phone into a pocket of his coat, and leaned back. "I thought you'd be getting ready fer the Scott Supper, yet here ye are."

"I'm about to leave."

"Are ye going tae join the lot on a permanent basis?"

"I'm not much of a joiner."

The inspector nodded knowingly. The two of us were cut from the same introverted cloth. Both left-handed, if that attests to anything, both cautious about allowing others into our lives, and we valued our own personal space. Although, while unable to speak for him, I really enjoy friends and meeting new people. Then I retreat, exhausted, to my cottage and Snookie, my Scottish Fold feline companion.

"Even Sean can quote Sir Walter Scott," I said, remembering Sean's recitation.

"*Silence, maiden; thy tongue outruns thy discretion,*" the inspector exclaimed with force. Several customers turned our way.

My mouth fell open. "Excuse…me?" Then realizing he was having fun with me, I replied, "Another Scott quote. Ill chosen, I might add."

The inspector chuckled, giving me a moment to searched my mind for a comeback. I had it, a snippet from the depths of my stored memories. "*A fool's wild speech confounds the wise,*" I recited.

He laughed out loud at that. So did several others, including Bill and Andy.

Musicians had been fussing with gear at a corner table and came forth with fiddles, beginning an impromptu fiddle session with *The Fairy Dance,* a lively reel that ended our conversation as we fixed our attention on the music.

I grinned, feeling warm and content, the pesky pages forgotten for the moment.

Chapter 2

Derrick and Brenda Findley lived on Crannog Lane in a traditional villa on slightly elevated ground, overlooking the village and Moray Firth, an inlet on the North Sea. I parked my Peugeot on the street below, Vicki exited from the passenger seat, and we followed a private path upward through mature trees, entering the vestibule after a warm welcome from the host and hostess. We wandered into the dining room to the music and lyrics of Caledonia, a song that made its appearance often at the pub.

I'd learned the words and silently sang along.

I have moved and I've kept on moving
proved the points that I needed proving
Lost the friends that I needed losing
found others on the way
I have tried and I've kept on trying
stolen dreams, yes there's no denying

I have traveled hard sometimes with conscience flying
somewhere in the wind

Momentarily, I found myself seated. The supper, served at a table beside an open hearth, was a formal affair; the men in Highland kilts and the women in their best finery. My go-to black dress was classic, and it worked well. Vicki, her blonde hair tied in a knot on top of her head, wore a tartan skirt, and her signature perfume with hints of rose and jasmine scenting the air.

There were eight of us, a smaller group that usual, according to Vicki, due to May holidays, which was why she and the other members had been strongly encouraged to invite guests. Recruiting new and young members was an ongoing concern with the aging club members.

Brenda and Derrick, with whom I was acquainted through the pub and small talk there, sat at opposite ends of the dining table, which I could see had room for expansion in additional leaves.

I also knew Stuart McKay from his readings at the bookstore. He was a retired university professor from Edinburgh and sat across from me, sporting a tartan kilt with shades of blue, a Prince Charlie kilt jacket, a black bow tie, leather sporran, argyle hose and ghillie brogues.

His kilt colors reminded me of my own. The Elliott tartan was a bold blue, crisscrossed with deep yellow stripes, while Stuart's was a much deeper blue with green plaid. Plaid was pronounced like 'played' by Scots.

A decorative knife was sheathed and tucked into the top of his hose, which brought legal rules and regulations to my mind. Weaponry of any sort was banned in Scotland. The general populace couldn't even carry pepper spray, a rule that didn't apply to me, thanks to my role as constable.

Whether because the knife was acceptable within a private setting or because Stuart was rather distinguished looking, no one had suggested that he remove it when he'd arrived. But perhaps concessions were allowed when donning this historical garb.

Vicki occupied the seat to my left. To my right sat Dr. Teague, our local general practitioner owning a small surgery in the village center. The doctor, in his late-forties, had bought out old Dr. Keen late last year, allowing the eighty-year-old to retire and move south to be closer to his family. Dr. Teague had dressed as formally as Stuart. I'd been to see him with a case of influenza during the winter, and I found him compassionate and capable.

Rounding up the eight were Dallas Irving, proprietor of the bookshop and current president of the Scott Club, and a red-haired, rather rotund, thirtyish woman introduced as Morag Lisle, who had been a last-minute addition after overhearing Dallas and Vicki speaking about the club event at the bookstore and soliciting an invitation.

"I literally begged to attend," Morag told us with sparkling eyes. "I majored in the classics and am an avid follower of Sir Walter Scott and took every class on him that I could find. You can imagine my excitement when I learned of this supper. Thank you so much for allowing me tae attend."

"We're all so glad tae have you as a guest," Dr. Teague relied, warmly, glancing my way and smiling. "We have our own celebrity author at the table with us tonight."

"Hardly literary material," I said, a bit uncomfortable with the attention, taking a sip from a glass of red wine that Derrick had poured for each of us.

Morag leaned in, her cheeks glowing. "What do you write?"

"Modern romance."

"And she's very, very good," Vicki added, beaming while she exaggerated my talents as only a true friend can. "She's a smash hit."

"I second that," Dallas said. "Her books fly off the shelves."

"Only because you talk them up," I replied before turning to Stuart. "I'm curious about your decorative knife," I said.

He reached beneath the table and brandished it for all to view. "Ah," he said, "ye mean my sgian-dubh."

The blade was about five inches long. The polished black handle caught a ray of light from the fireplace and gleamed.

"Sheath it, please," Derrick demanded coldly, putting down his wine glass. "Ye know the custom is tae leave such things at the door. We made an exception fer ye based on yer dress, but will ask ye to remove it from the table, if necessary."

Stuart continued as though he hadn't heard Derrick, a smirk on his face, "The spear-point tip was handy for eatin' and preparin' meats. The blade is German steel. I keep it sharp and at the ready."

"Stuart?" Brenda said, firmly. "Enough."

With a shrug, Stuart returned it to the sheath at the top of his hose.

"Stuart," said Derrick, "I have somewhat o' a problem and need tae speak with ye about it. Do you think ye could stay after fer a private word?"

"A nightcap, fer my troubles," Stuart said with anticipation, "and I'll give ye any advice ye need."

The meal progressed with small talk and without the haggis I'd expected. We began with a crab and rice soup called partan bree followed by salmon from the North Sea caught fresh first thing this morning and a mashed potato, cheese, and cabbage dish called rumbledethumps.

"I expected that we'd have haggis," I mentioned, finding all of it delicious.

"Not likely. Haggis is served up at another type of gathering - Burns Nights," Stuart said, rather smugly, pouring another glass of wine. "*Address to a Haggis* is a Robert Burns' poem, and that is an entirely different event, so haggis isn't appropriate fer a Scott supper. They met, ye know."

"Burns and Scott met?" I asked, realizing the limitations of my Scottish novelist education.

"When Scott was but a lad. In the winter of 1787 when Scott would have been fifteen-years-old or thereaboots. The chance meeting influenced Scott's later career, made him what he became."

Dr. Teague scoffed. "Of course, the meeting influenced him beyond measure. That encounter was a turning point in his career. Robert Burns is Scotland's National Bard. No one has been able to match his contributions. Not even Scott."

"That's preposterous," Stuart fairly bellowed, coloring as though he'd been personally insulted. "Sir Walter Scott is the most influential novelist tae ever pick up pen in the whole o' Scotland."

"A rank below, is my thought," Dr. Teague replied, his voice and demeanor growing agitated. "I have a right tae state my opinion, even if it differs from yer own. Scott worshipped Burns. What was it he said once when someone offered up a comparison, *There is no comparison whatever*," he'd stated. "*We ought not to be named in the same day.*"

"I know their history," Stuart shot back.

"No need tae argue," Derrick said. "Both novelists were literary giants."

I glanced around the table. Morag's face registered discomfort, her bubbly enthusiasm diminished. Brenda scowled at her husband. Dallas busied herself with sips of wine, her eyes flitting over artwork on the wall.

Vicki met my gaze, sighed heavily, and stood up. "I'll fetch dessert. It's tipsy laird," she said, clearly wishing to stop the argument before it got out of hand.

"Brilliant idea," Dallas exclaimed. "I'll help serve."

The women disappeared into the kitchen. Before the contention at the table suppressed what was left of my appetite, I'd been looking forward to sampling Vicki's whisky trifle. Maybe dessert would return the table to equilibrium.

Stuart snorted, still smoldering. "Ye are an ignorant man!" he said to the doctor.

"Ignorant?" Dr. Teague sprang to his feet. "Name calling, are ye, Stuart. Over such a silly thing. And before we even have heard yer pathetic excuse fer a recitation. Go on, deliver it before ye have so much whisky ye slur yer words."

Stuart banged his fist on the table. "Callin' me a drunk, are ye? Let me remind ye that my blade is sharp!"

"Pished, ye are tae threaten me." Dr. Teague turned to Derrick. "Thank ye fer hosting, but I'll be on my way. I won't stay and be threatened by the likes of him."

"Please don't go," Brenda begged.

"Dessert will be served shortly," Derrick added.

In spite of the host and hostess' protests, the doctor stormed out.

"Good riddance," Stuart snarled, with what appeared to be malicious satisfaction.

Morag rose quickly to her feet, practically sending her chair over backwards.
"Ah...I...ah...best be off. And thank ye, Brenda, fer having me. And tell Dallas thank you fer the invite."

Morag departed on the doctor's heels moments before Vicki and Dallas appeared with dessert.

"What happened to the others?" Vicki asked then quickly went on, "Well, never mind that."

Brenda worried a string of pearls around her neck, perfectly aware that the evening was sliding into ruin.

It wasn't a complete disaster though. The tipsy laird was as wonderful as I'd imagined it would be. The trifle was layered with sponge cake, custard, a dash of whisky, and raspberries, then adorned with flaked almonds. A true thing of beauty as well as a culinary delight.

And, although Stuart had presented a bad showing earlier, his delivery of an excerpt from *The Lady of the Lake* was superb.

Shortly after, Vicki and I departed with Dallas. Stuart stayed as Derrick had requested earlier assuming he had been specially chosen for a nightcap.

"Stuart can be a bit condescending," I pointed out as we followed the path down to the street.

"A bit?" Vicki quipped. "And Doc Teague went out of his way to provoke him. Those two have been at each other's throats for the last several meetings. It's time to take action." She glanced at the president of the club, waiting for Dallas to agree.

"Stuart is a brilliant scholar of Scott's life and works," Dallas said instead, defending him. "But he does tend to the pompous side, a wee bit grating on the nerves and the doctor doesn't help the matter by goading him. I'll speak to both of them. I'm afraid the two of them scared away Morag with their sharp words. I doubt she'll be back. And you, Eden? Please don't say this is yer last supper with us?"

"It takes more than an over-inflated egotistical college prof and a doctor who knows how to push buttons to frighten me away," I replied, opening the door of my Peugeot and sliding in as Vicki climbed into the passenger seat.

Arriving home, I was still wound up from the evening so I joined my friend in her home. Moments later, Sean's police vehicle pulled up. I lingered long enough for a recap of the evening, Vicki and I recounting the altercation between the two men for Sean's benefit. Right around eleven o'clock, I wished them good night and walked over to my own cottage.

I greeted Snookie and changed into a nightgown while Snookie wound around my legs, purring. We settled on the bed, and I pulled the quilt up close to my ears, considering whether or not to read for a bit.

Before I could decide, my phone rang.

"Get yerself up," Jamieson said from the other end. "There's been a murder. Sean's already on the way."

The location of the scene of the crime chilled me to the bone.

Chapter 3

Crannog Lane had been cordoned off. I had to park several blocks away and walk. As I approached, I could see a blow-up tent at the foot of the path leading to Derrick and Brenda Findlay's home. Jamieson was waiting and grimly spoke to one of the officers guarding the perimeter, approving my passing under the white and blue barrier tape.

The victim's identity was still unknown to me since the inspector had refused to stay on the line once my presence had been requested and the address imparted. He'd ended the call abruptly, leaving me with growing concerns.

Was the victim Derrick? Or Brenda?

But as I walked toward the tent, both of them were standing off to the side, speaking with Sean.

"I ken ye have yer own version o' the evening," Jamieson said to me. "And I want tae hear it once we're finished here. The body o' Stuart McKay is inside the tent."

"Stuart?" But I suspected as much once I'd noted that the Findlay's were in attendance. Stuart had been the last of us to leave, lingering with the host and hostess at Derrick's request.

"Are we through with the Findlay's fer now?" Sean called to Jamieson.

"You're free tae go, but we will have more questions later."

Brenda and Derrick turned and slowly made their way up the path. Sean joined us.

"The Findlay's told me about the argument during supper between the doctor and the victim," the inspector said to me.

"Their version matched yers and Vicki's from yer accounts last night," Sean added.

"The discussion became heated, but certainly not murder-worthy," I replied. "Dr. Teague left rather abruptly after Stuart referred to him as an ignorant man."

"Maybe their exchange isn't a proper motive in yer own mind," Sean replied. "But who can tell what goes on in the mind of criminal elements."

"But he's our village physician," I insisted, sounding naïve even to my own ears. "He's sworn an oath. The Hippocratic Oath." I turned to Jamieson. "Dr. Teague couldn't have done this, could he?"

"Let's not get ahead o' ourselves before we haff the facts." The inspector's eyes were cold and sharp. "Do ye want tae take a look inside the tent?"

I'd rather not, was on the tip of my tongue, but if I ever wanted to excel in my position, and I truly did, then I needed to handle situations like this with strength and awareness. Besides, as I reminded myself, this wouldn't be my first stabbing victim. The other one that I'd encountered had brought me to the inspector's attention and to this job.

I followed Jamieson, stooping to step inside, where one of the forensic team members was packing up.

Stuart's torso was covered with black plastic. His eyes were sightless, the smugness and self-assuredness gone. Instead, an expression of shocked disbelief was etched permanently into his face.

"He was stabbed in the heart," Jamieson said at my side. "A direct hit. Either very lucky or the attacker knew what he or she was about."

"Where is the murder weapon?" I asked.

"It isn't here. I have officers combing the neighborhood in case it was dropped hereabouts."

My eyes traveled to Stuart's legs jutting out from the plastic, to the top of his argyles. "The knife he carried is missing."

"Aye, the holster in his stocking was a tipoff that he'd had a sgian-dubh on his person. The Findlay's confirmed the fact, along with relating the threat he'd made tae Dr. Teague."

Things weren't looking good for the doctor. With a squabble only a few hours before. Now one of them dead, thanks to a professional thrust to the heart. And Dr. Teague, a skilled medical professional. He'd need a rock-solid alibi to redirect the focus of the inspector's investigation.

The tent's walls began closing in on me, the air turning repressive. I abruptly turned and made my way outside, relishing the fresh air. The inspector stayed inside.

"I'll need tae question ye," Sean said, writing in a notebook, puffed up with importance. "And Vicki, o' course. And the book lady. And that other one. And learn where each o' ye were at the time o' the murder. The boss wants tae handle the doctor." Sean flipped a page in his pad, scanning his notes. "According tae Derrick Findlay, the victim departed shortly after Vicki and yerself. And he dinnae make it far, as ye can see."

"Vicki and I drove home together around ten o'clock, as you well know." The over-eager new cop could be exasperating at times. Really? He needed to know where I was at the time of the murder? "The three of us were together until shortly before the inspector called informing us of the murder. You. Vicki. Me. We have alibis."

"I knew that. Just being thorough."

"Stuart's murder might not have anything to do with the supper or with the doctor," I suggested. "Perhaps Stuart entered the street at the wrong time and saw something he shouldn't have. A robbery gone bad perhaps." A thought occurred to me. "That car robber. Maybe Stuart saw an attack in progress and tried to intercede."

"Could o' happened," Sean agreed, bobbing his head.

Only where was the targeted pensioner? Had the panic-stricken woman driven off, leaving Stuart to fight for his life? Maybe. If that were the case, hopefully she would report it soon.

"Who found the body?" I wanted to know.

"Cabbie driving past, saw a form on the sidewalk, and pulled over. Must o' been right after the attack. We have a very small window of time here, and that's going tae help us. The perpetrator shoulda killed Stuart out o' public view tae gain more time."

"Looks to me like his attacker gained plenty of time, since we don't have a suspect in custody."

Jamieson stepped out of the tent, returning his cell phone to a clip on his belt. "I'm afraid yer statement will have tae wait, Constable Elliott. It appears that the Pensioner Robber has struck again. This time out on Laurel Crescent."

"I'll take this one, too," Sean said. "I'm on my way."

"Constable Elliott goes with ye."

Sean was already hurrying away. "Meet me at me beat car," he called to me. "And hurry yerself up."

"And Eden," the inspector said. "Don't let him mess this up."

"A little faith, Inspector."

"Chust keep an eye on him."

*

Laurel Crescent was a poorly lit street that led into a quiet residential area directly off the main artery from Glenkillen to Inverness, a perfect place to commit a crime without witnesses. A grey Vauxhall Corsa sat off the road in the dark shadow of a silver birch tree with a Highland patrol car parked behind it. On our approach, one of the officers stepped out of the patrol car's passenger side. His partner in the driver's seat appeared to be writing a report.

We showed the officer our credentials.

"My partner and I came upon this car here," he told us. "Almost missed it off the road like that and no street lights tae help. On closer inspection, we found the victim in the boot, none the worse fer wear, but missing a handbag and mobile."

"The Pensioner Robber strikes again," Sean said. "Twice in less than twenty-four hours."

"She'd been in the boot over three hours," the officer informed us.

Sean wrote something in his notebook. "Steppin' it up, he is. Getting careless."

"Can we speak to the woman?" I asked.

"I'll turn the entire situation over tae ye," the officer said, opening the rear door of the patrol car. "We patrol the main thoroughfare. We only happened on the car while doing a turnaround. This one is yours."

To my surprise, Morag Lisle crawled out of the backseat.

"Morag!" I exclaimed. "What happened?"

"Eden!" She practically fell into my arms.

The officer interrupted before he stepped back into the patrol car. "A reunion it tis then. We'll be on our way."

I untangled myself from Morag and we watched them speed away.

"Ye know each other from the supper," Sean said, scribbling away. "I recognize yer name. Here it is. Morag Lisle."

I quickly related the details of our meeting, since last night's conversation with Sean and Vicki had mostly centered around the two dueling men. When I finished, Morag added to my story.

"As ye know, I left the supper right behind the doctor. I'm renting a room in a bungalow a little further up Laurel Crescent. I'd turned off the main road when a figure came out o' the shadow, right in front of my car. At first, I thought it was a deer, but by the time I realized it was a person, my driver door was flung open. I didn't have a chance tae escape. He took my belongings and forced me into the boot at knifepoint."

"Sean," I asked, "was the last victim a pensioner?"

"Aye."

Sean and I exchanged glances. This was the second such occurrence, with the robber rushing his victim's automobile and forcing her into the car's trunk. The only difference was in Morag's age. She certainly wasn't a senior citizen. The robber was changing things up significantly.

"Can you describe the knife he used?" I asked, realizing that this attack had to have occurred prior to Stuart's murder, while he was carrying his in his stocking and sitting cockily at the supper table.

Morag shrugged. "Silver blade, about this long." She extended her index fingers, indicating approximately three inches, several inches shorter than the kilt knife.

"What did the robber look like?"

"Dark jogging bottoms, had on one o' those face masks like ye see bank robbers wear on television."

"That's him, all right," Sean said. "What was in yer handbag?"

"Credit card, draft card, a few pounds—normal purse items. This has been a traumatic experience fer me." She rubbed her forehead. "I can't think straight right now to come up with an inventory."

"You are going to have to answer some questions," I said, gently. "Then Sean will try to track your phone."

"I need tae go tae my place," Morag insisted. "I have tae notify my card issuers immediately."

Sean stepped in, "Ye can do that in a bit. There has been a murder and your presence is required here, right now."

"A murder?"

Sean hesitated, pleading eyes focused on me. There was no easy way to say it, so I plunged on, "Stuart McKay was found stabbed to death on the street outside Brenda and Derrick Findlay's home. Inspector Jamieson will want to get a statement from you."

After a stunned moment, Morag said, "Oh my God, That's terrible. I wish I'd never asked fer an invitation to that supper! Trapped in the boot of my own car fer hours, and now this! And here it is the middle of the night. I never met any of you before tonight, don't know anything that might be of help." Morag's jawline tightened. "A statement will have to wait until tomorrow."

Sean took up the challenge. "I'm afraid it can't wait. Tis a murder, woman. I'll put ye in handcuffs if I have tae."

Morag sighed. "Since ye put it that way, it appears that I have no choice. But ye know we all saw and heard the same thing. It's going tae be repetitious and a waste o' time."

And she was partly right. My account of the evening matched hers up to the point when she left the supper, as later did Dallas' and Vicki's. Although those two had missed the doctor's and Morag's departures while serving up tipsy laird.

It seemed like forever before we were finished and I drove to my cottage, wondering how the inspector had faired with Dr. Teague.

As rays of sun cleared the horizon, announcing a new day, I fell into bed where my feline companion curled waiting and slept hard and dreamless.

Chapter 4

Late morning, and I awoke to find Snookie wrapping her soft white body around the top of my head, purring contently, not a care in the world. Coffee, a shower, and fresh clothing, and I felt almost human again. Strolling down the lane past Vicki's house, I encountered more members of our animal menagerie. Sheep dotted the hillsides, overseen by the farm's herding dogs, and the barn was home to Jasper, our feral cat, who was sometimes friendly, but only on his terms.

He stalked nonchalantly over to where I'd stopped and wound between my legs, arching and stretching. Next, Vicki's two West Highland terriers raced up for attention. Pepper and Coco crowded each other as I bent to stroke them in fair distribution.

Beyond, I could see Sheep Expressions, the farm's wool and yarn shop, which is popular with visitors and has become a frequent tour bus stop.

Vicki would be there preparing for knitting classes or restocking shelves, immersing herself in a kaleidoscope of colors and softness.

Idyllic. Where life slows down. My haven. I like to think that the ugliness of the world can't touch me here. Today, more than any other day, I wanted to remain on the farm, forget about the murder, and pretend that Dr. Teague wasn't the prime suspect. Unfortunately, as a constable, my wish would not be granted. How had this atrocity occurred? And more importantly, why?

Sun shone from above, but an invisible cloud formed over me as I contemplated the most likely outcome. Our village's esteemed doctor convicted of first-degree murder. Over a dispute regarding two literary giants. A difference of opinion hardly seemed a motive for murder. There had to be more to it.

What had Vicki said as we left the gathering?

That the two of them had been at each other's throats before. We'd have to find out the real reason for their animosity toward each other. And the place to start was with the survivor. The Doctor. Jamieson would have grilled him thoroughly by now. The inspector didn't sleep much during a case, as I'd become aware of during past criminal investigations.

Speaking of the relentless inspector, my cell phone chimed, informing me that Jamieson was trying to contact me.

"Do *not* wish me a good morning," he snarled before I even opened my mouth. I hated speaking with him early in the morning and as usual, I considered ignoring his call until later when he wasn't so crabby. Wishful thinking on my part. I couldn't bring myself to let his calls go to messaging.

"What is it that you want then?" I replied matching his tone.

"I've sent Sean tae get ye. And make it quick. Time's wastin'."

"I'm on my way to speak with Vicki about a few things I forgot to ask earlier, regarding previous confrontations between Stuart and the doctor." I was already standing on the steps leading into Sheep Expressions. "This won't take long."

Sean's patrol car appeared down the lane, traveling my way.

"Get yerself here, Constable. And that's an order. Besides, yer Vicki doesn't know anything useful."

"Where is here?" I wanted to know, but he'd hung up.

Agitated by the inspector's bullish behavior, nevertheless, I slid into the patrol car beside Sean and immediately asked, "What's going on?

"'Tis not fer the likes of us tae know, it seems. I feel like pullin' a hair from his nose."

In spite of my irritation over Jamieson's brisk summons, I had to smile. "Pull one for me, too," I replied, noting that we were winding through the center of the village, heading west. "Where are we going?"

"Tae the boss' house. He gave me directions."

"Really." This was interesting. I'd never been there before. The man was usually extremely private and as far as I was aware, didn't entertain guests, and especially not his team. Which led to the next question. "Why?"

"We'll find out soon enough."

So, Sean didn't know any more than I did. "Any luck tracking Morag's phone?"

Ahead, a red deer leapt across the narrow road followed by another and Sean slowed in case there were more. "Like all the rest of the stolen mobiles. Tossed in a garbage bin. Hers was in one close tae the scene o' the bugger's crime."

"Witnesses?"

45

"Not a one, at least none that will admit tae it."

We sped up, took another turn, then another, and grazing fields turned quickly into woodlands. Finally, we arrived in a clearing surrounded by pines and junipers, where we parked on a stone drive and climbed out of the vehicle.

"Tis a hunting box," Sean informed me, while I took in my surroundings, particularly interested in the inspector's choice of home.

A box? I'd never heard the reference before. In the states, we'd call this dwelling a lodge. Or a cabin. I studied the wood exterior, which was rather plain, while Sean walked up to the door and opened it.

"You better knock," I advised him, thinking my suggestion would save him a cursing.

"Boss said tae come right in."

The simple exterior had deceived me into thinking the interior would be plain also. Instead, the cozy interior was all pine walls, wood floors, and banks of windows. Jamieson sat in a leather chair beside a picture window with a stunning view of the forest. I was drawn to the sight of colorful goldfinches and tits jostling for perches on a bird feeder.

Reluctantly turning from the view, I noticed that the inspector's left leg was raised, resting on a footstool and supported by pillows. Crutches leaned against the wall within arm's reach.

"I fell off the curb beside the crime scene and can't put weight on the bloody ankle," he said, with a grimace of pain.

"Have you been to the doctor?" I asked, glancing at the crutches.

"Ye mean to our star suspect fer tending?" Jamieson growled. "I didn't even get a chance tae go tae his home and question him before I did this stupid thing. I've been icing it and wrapped it. That'll have tae do fer now. And the crutches were in my attic, old things, they are. Take a seat, both o' ye."

Sean plopped down on the sofa, and I joined him.

"Smart thinking on yer part tae avoid our local doctor." Sean said, "If the doc is our killer, he might o' shot ye up with poison, and then we'd have a dead boss on our hands and a double murder."

"Thank ye fer pointing that out," Jamieson said to him. "If yer done with wild speculations, we

47

have work tae do. Constable Stevens, ye need tae canvass in the vicinity o' last night's robbery, find us a witness, anybody who saw anything out o' place. And I expect ye tae do better than ye haff been with finding clues to apprehending the Pensioner Robber."

I chimed in, "We might want to rename him. His latest victim was Morag Lisle, and she's a long way from retirement age." I filled him in on the latest heist.

"He's branching out." Sean added. "And maybe he's addin' murder tae his list of crimes."

Jamieson looked annoyed. "If ye thought it through, ye'd ask yerself questions and ponder findin' the proper answers right in front o' yer nose. Fer example, if he did in fact attack Stuart McKay and leave him dead on the street, he changed his methods tae the extreme. The victim wasn't inside an auto, nor was he feeble. He was a solid built man, not some weakened old woman. And he was wearing a kilt and traditional weaponry. Hardly a vulnerable target. Our robber is more o' a coward than that."

"It was just an idea," Sean admitted, deflating. "And now eliminated."

"Stuart might have interrupted the robbery," I suggested. At the flash in the inspector's eyes, cold and sharp as daggers themselves, I hastily added. "Whoever was the real target may have been afraid and drove away as soon as the attacker turned from her to Stuart. It's a possibility, no matter how slim."

The inspector slowly lowered his foot to the floor and fumbled for the crutches. "And what about the knife? Although the medical report isn't ready, the M.E. says that the blade wound is consistent with a knife such as Stuart's. The robber had his own. Why use Stuart's, then run off with it?"

I didn't have an answer for that.

The inspector dropped one of his crutches and frowned. "I've issued a request, asking motorists tae check their webcam footage both out at Laurel Crescent and in the village fer several blocks surrounding the murder scene, as we've done fer all the robberies. With a bit o' luck, something will show up."

I picked up the crutch and handed it to him. He tucked it under his arm and glared at Sean. "So, what are ye waitin' fer? Give it some stick!"

Sean jumped to his feet and for a moment, I thought he might salute. Instead, he fairly shouted, "Aye, sir!" and headed for the door.

"Wait for me," I warned him. "You're my ride!"

"Never mind that." Jamieson waved him off. "I'll see that she gets back."

Sean disappeared, and I turned to find the inspector chuckling.

"You enjoy harassing poor Sean," I said, realizing how difficult it was to tell what his mood really was at any given moment. "And what in the world does 'give it some stick' mean?"

"Put some energy into it. That's all. What? Ye don't have that expression where ye come from?"

I shook my head. "Hardly. But let's put some stick into it ourselves. I think we should get you to the doctor."

"My thought exactly." Jamieson, unfamiliar with operating crutches, made an awkward start. "I trust ye'll prevent the good doctor from poisoning me."

"Depends," I said, trailing slowly behind as we approached his Honda CR-V.

"On what?"

"On your behavior. I'm going to ask him about putting you on anti-cranky pills though."

"This injury had tae happen tae my drivin' foot and force me tae depend on ye, of all people."

I held the door for him. "Now you're stuck with me."

"Aye, that I am."

As he grappled with the crutches, cursing under his breath, I realized that I was just as stuck with the inspector as he was with me.

And how would we handle that?

Chapter 5

The surgery was located two blocks from the pub. On the way over, Jamieson reiterated what the medical examiner had shared with him regarding direct heart strikes, information I could have lived my entire life without needing to know.

"'Tis hard tae stab the heart itself," he explained. "The heart lies behind the sternum, protected by ribs and tough connective tissue. Usually, a major artery is hit instead, death resulting from massive internal bleeding. Either the attacker would have tae have incredible upper body strength tae penetrate the ribs or have a keen grasp o' the human skeletal system. The strike was between the fourth and fifth rib, with the knife angled into the left ventricle."

I thought about that, unwanted images of Stuart's last moments forming in my mind. "The attacker meant business."

"Aye, almost like an execution. If this person had been the car robber surprised in the act, he would o' been fightin' tae escape, not aiming tae kill. If he did try tae murder our victim, it would o' been easier fer him tae go fer the kidneys or stomach."

"You've convinced me that they aren't one and the same," I replied.

"And here's another important detail when stabbing fer the heart." His piercing eyes met mine briefly when I shifted my vision from the road. "The most damage tae the heart is done with the point o' the knife," he said. "It has tae be extremely sharp."

Eyes back on the road, I said, "And Stuart's certainly was. He made sure everyone knew that."

"The guests at the table will be our focus unless something presents itself tae lead us in a different direction."

After parking and getting the inspector upright and moving, we entered the surgery and sat in the waiting room while Dr. Teague finished with a patient. The advantage of having a village physician is the freedom to wander in at will, rather than always needing to schedule an appointment days or weeks in advance. Once the patient left, the doctor locked the door and reversed the open sign. Closed. Teague knew why we were here.

"I see yer favoring yer leg," he said, noting the crutches beside Jamieson.

"My ankle hasn't cooperated since I turned it last night."

"I have a meeting soon, but I have time tae take a look," he said, and we followed him into an exam room. "Up on the examining table with ye after ye remove yer shoe and sock. Ye don't mind Eden remaining in the room during the exam?"

"Her presence is necessary, I'm afraid." Jamieson did as he'd been asked.

"This is more than a medical visit, I presume. I heard about Stuart this morning. It was a shock, ye ken."

He examined the ankle, gently applying light pressure.

"Is it broken?" I asked, imagining long weeks of caregiving in my future rather than a few days.

"An X-ray is needed. Eden, if ye'll step out fer a moment. It won't take but a minute."

I paged through a magazine until I was called back in for the verdict.

"Not fractured, so that's good," the doctor said. "It's likely sprained. I'll wrap it fer ye, although ye did a good job on yer own."

"A sprain? I could o' diagnosed that myself," the inspector grumbled, perfecting the bad patient. "I didn't need an X-ray."

I gave him my best warning stare.

While the doctor tended to Jamieson's ankle, he asked for details of the murder.

"Ye know I can't talk about an ongoing investigation," the inspector replied. "And it's me that needs tae question yerself. Where did ye go when ye left the Findlay's last night?"

The doctor finished and I thought his face was a bit pale, although he had to have anticipated some sort of interrogation. "I went to the Kilt & Thistle fer some peace and quiet and a pint, and tae try tae salvage the evening best I could. Nobody likes tae speak ill of the dead, but Stuart was intolerable. The rare occasion when the man wasn't presenting the hot-headed side of his personality, he was hangin' his bum out the window, talking nonsense."

The inspector nodded an acknowledgement rather than agreement. "How long were ye at the pub?"

"Not long as the place was crowded with an overnight group of tourists on a bus who were staying next door at the inn."

"And after that?"

"I came here. My flat is above the surgery. I prepared fer today by goin' over my schedule and then went tae bed."

The inspector scowled. "Anyone tae vouch fer ye?"

Dr. Teague shrugged. "I'm known by the pub owner, Dale. He was tending bar. After that…well…I live alone." He stepped back. "Ye can step down, but easy. Take most o' the weight on yer other foot."

While the inspector put on his sock and shoe, I continued with a few of my own questions. "You didn't get along with the deceased. That was obvious."

"He needles me, seems tae want tae show me up as inferior tae him." A look of sadness crossed his face. "Or rather, he needled me, past tense. I can't get used tae the fact that he is gone. Stuart was a nasty bloke, but he didn't deserve tae die like that. I've suspected he had a poor sense o' self in spite of all his bluster."

An interesting observation by the doctor.

"Ye need tae stay off that ankle," he advised Jamieson. "Keep using the crutches, and ye'll heal faster. Ice it morning, night, and some in between, and let me know how yer doin' in a few days."

Then he addressed both of us. "I came here from Glasgow after well over a decade as a highly skilled surgeon. The fast pace, the city life, it wears on a chap after a while. When this surgery came up fer sale, I jumped at the chance. Ye know why?"

Jamieson waited silently. I shook my head.

"I appreciated the ruralness of it and the idea of a general practice. And instead of doing the same thing day in and day out, my days are enormously varied. One day at the scene of a road accident. Another attending tae a home birth. I enjoy walking down the street and greeting patients. That never happened in Glasgow."

He smiled. "At the pub last night, someone told me how lucky Glenkillen is tae have a good doctor living in the village. That made me feel grand."

"I like it here, too," I told him as we entered the waiting room. "Such a feeling of community."

"Now that we've established that the village is tae both o' yer likings," the inspector growled, "ye say ye were a skilled surgeon. Performing operations in hospital settings, I imagine."

"Aye." The doctor looked nervous for the first time since we'd begun questioning him. "I can see where ye are going with this, with the two of us arguing only hours before and my background in surgery. But ye don't need tae be an expert tae lop off a bloke's head."

"What?" the inspector fairly roared. "Where did you hear that bit o' poppycock?"

"From one o' my patients," the doctor answered. "Seems cause of death is well known. Not a surprise, considering the size of Glenkillen."

"Stuart McKay wasn't beheaded," Jamieson corrected him. "He was stabbed in the heart."

"Directly in the heart," I added.

The doctor slowly sat down in one of the chairs. "It looks bad fer me then."

Neither Jamieson nor I replied since the question was rhetorical in nature. The inspector pressed on, "I'd like tae know how ye felt during yer disagreement with McKay?"

"You mean, did I think about killing him? Of course, not."

"But ye were angry?"

"Yes, but I didn't kill him."

"Then who at that table do ye think might have?"

Dr. Teague's brows knit. "Why are you assuming that Stuart's murderer was at our supper?"

"Tis as good a place as any tae start. Do you think one o' the women did it? Eden here or Vicki? How about the village bookseller, or the reader who found out and joined at the last minute? Or the hosts?"

That seemed to jog something in the doctor's memory. "Ye might talk tae Derrick," he said. "Not that he'd murder anybody. But ye might find that I wasn't the only one who had an issue with Stuart. Derrick had warned him after the last meeting tae behave better or tae be forced out of the club. He'd had fair warning. I was more than a wee bit surprised that the pompous braggart didn't follow Derrick's advice. I'd hoped tae have a peaceful supper."

I remembered that Vicki had mentioned prior clashes between them. "The two of you have had words at other club events?"

"Nothing more significant than the disagreeable chat over Scott and Burns. Always small stuff. I should have kept quiet, but the man irritated me and I joined right in."

Jamieson tucked the crutches under his arms. I opened the door. "I'll have more questions fer ye in the immediate future," he warned. "Ye aren't planning any getaways, are ye?"

The doctor sighed in resignation. "No, my practice keeps me right here. And the implication isn't going unnoticed."

"As intended," the inspector said under his breath. "After this meeting o' yers, stop at the station tae make yer statement."

Out on the street, the day had warmed. Jamieson struggled to get into the passenger seat of his vehicle, knocking the crutches about until finally managing to get them wedged between the seats, while I raised my face to the sun, tempted to run off.

"Don't chust stand there," he ordered. "Get in."

I turned to him, having become increasingly annoyed with his attitude. "You need to treat me with more respect, if you want me to drive you."

"Blast it!" And he slammed the door.

Chapter 6

Street parking outside the Kilt & Thistle was limited. I dropped the inspector at the door and searched for a parking space. After finding one, I made my way to the pub and noticed a Vauxhall Corsa parked in front that matched the appearance of the one belonging to Morag Lisle. Before entering the pub, a piano riff text message came in from Ami, and I paused to read it.

"Vicki sent a message claiming that the two of you were involved in a murder!!!" That was so like Ami to line up multiple exclamation points behind a sentence.

Ever since Vicki and Ami became pen pals through messaging and emailing, my movements weren't as private as they once had been. "Not exactly, as in suspects," I replied, "but had been dining with the victim before his death. I'm assisting Jamieson with the investigation."

"Exactly how closely are you working with the inspector?" came back the question from the famous historical romance writer. The woman with a one-track mind. At least she wasn't focusing on Leith at the moment. "I can imagine you with an older man. Yes, clearly, I can."

"Got to go interrogate a suspect," I shot back.

"Carry handcuffs and don't be afraid to use them!!!"

I tucked the phone into a pocket, with a smile at Ami's reference to handcuffs, sexual as usual. Now that my friend had mentioned them, why hadn't I been authorized for handcuffs? I'd bring it up at the proper time.

Entering the pub, I found Jamieson drinking coffee at the bar's counter. "I ordered two bowls o' Scotch broth," he told me. "Assumed you were hungry."

"Great."

Scotch broth is a filling soup much like the American version of beef and barley, although lamb is often used instead of beef. The Kilt & Thistle's version was also rich with split peas and leeks.

Before I seated myself on the chair next to him, I scanned the tables, wondering if I'd correctly identified the car outside as Morag's.

Bill Morris and Andy occupied Bill's regular table. Both had coffee cups in front of them, but I would have bet Bill had flavored his with a nip of whisky. Bill saw me and gave me a nod, then scowled at the inspector's back, indicating his disapproval, an ongoing wariness when it came to Jamieson, as I knew from past encounters between them.

Morag did indeed occupy a table, and she wasn't alone, either. In fact, I was acquainted with her fellow pub mates, as well.

"Did you notice that back table?" I fairly hissed to Jamieson. But he didn't reply since our soup was being delivered at the moment by Dale, the owner of the Kilt & Thistle.

"What can I get fer ye tae drink, Eden?" he asked.

"Coffee, please."

I was as hot as the coffee Dale poured and placed in front of me before he went off to serve others.

"Did you see who is over there?" I asked again.

"Take up yer spoon and let's eat in peace."

"They're all from the Scott Supper! Dallas, Morag, Derrick, and Brenda!"

"Aye, except fer Vicki, the doctor, and yerself. Weren't ye invited?"

"No, I wasn't." I took the seat beside him, sitting sideways, and shifting my eyes their way. "What are they doing? Comparing notes on the evening?"

"Most likely. Eat yer soup."

"Is that legal?"

"O' course it's legal. What do ye think I should do about it? Arrest them fer congregating?"

"At the very least it should bother you as much as it does me."

I sipped some of the broth not really tasting it; upset to find club members banding together right after one of them had been murdered. And why hadn't I been apprised of this get-together?

I'd had my fair share of exclusions at different periods in my life and it always was emotionally painful. Unpleasant memories flooded back to me. Mean girls, traveling in packs and verbally stabbing those of us who were more introverted. Gym classes, teams picked, always one of the last selected. I shook the images away and began to eat my soup in earnest.

The inspector turned and studied me; his spoon poised above his bowl. "A celebrated author ye were when first ye met them fer the supper," he stated, kindly. "Now yer a cop tae be avoided."

"Vicki isn't over there, either."

"Because she's yer good friend. And she's engaged tae a police officer. Therefore, chust as distrustful in their eyes."

I swiveled for another look. I caught Dallas' eye, her expression nervous and embarrassed. She leaned forward and spoke to her comrades. Brenda swiveled her head my way. I gave a weak wave.

"I really was excluded intentionally," I muttered, perfectly capable of reading between the lines even without the inspector's astute observations.

"They've formed a connection over the murder," he said gently. "Stronger than their bond through the reading club. It's not an uncommon occurrence after something as traumatic as a murder."

With his hunger satisfied, Jamieson's attitude had vastly improved. With a nourishing meal, Mr. Hyde had transformed into Dr. Jekyll.

He even chuckled when he said, "You don't want tae hang with that gossipy lot anyway." Then his eyes slid to the door. "Well, look who else has arrived. If it isn't the good doctor."

I spun to see which path Teague would take, curious to know whether he'd choose to join us at the bar or if he'd had a prior invitation to the table.

The inspector spoke to the doctor, "So that group over there is the meeting ye said ye were tae attend."

While Dallas had appeared sheepish, Dr. Teague's expression was defiant. "No law against having a quiet meal with friends."

"Yer right about that. Enjoy it." The inspector turned back to me, the conversation at an end.

The doctor joined the others, and we went on to finish our soup in silence, while I strained to hear fragments of their conversation. Nothing stood out clearly over the din of the pub.

"We have their statements, other than the doctor's, and that's comin' today," Jamieson pointed out. "All o' them were questioned separately before any o' them showed up here. They aren't plotting. They're sharing in their grief and looking fer answers. Whatever they're banging on about will come out, if it's important tae the case." The inspector glanced in the direction of the table then turned back to me. "In fact, I say, let them talk amongst themselves. Maybe one o' them, if the killer is in their midst, will say too much."

His eyes went directly to the doctor, who was speaking earnestly to Dallas. Six months earlier, I would have wondered why the man wasn't already in jail, considering what had transpired between him and the deceased, and Teague's lack of an alibi. But I'm slightly more experienced these days. Arresting a suspect is easy, getting a conviction is not. This investigation would be a slow process, but the inspector was a patient man and would see it through.

"Personally, I like the doctor," I said.

"Do ye think all criminals are nasty sorts on the surface? That they can't put up a good front?"

Before I could answer, Dale arrived with more fresh, hot coffee.

"Was Dr. Teague in yer establishment last night?" The inspector asked him.

"Aye, it was a busy night. It's good tae have a tour bus stop fer the night, but I like tae see them go as well."

"What time was the doctor here?" I inserted myself.

Dale frowned in thought. "It was right busy, uh, around eight, if I have tae guess. And I'm also guessing this is in regard tae Stuart McKay."

"Did ye notice when he left?" The inspector asked.

"He dinnae stay long; said it was a bit noisy fer him. Is the doc in trouble?"

Jamieson shifted. "Chust confirming his whereaboots as we are with many others."

Soon after, Andy Morris edged in next to us. "Is it true that…that Stuart McKay was beheaded? That's the scuttle around the village." His voice carried like a foghorn. Conversations slowed, then ceased.

Jamieson's face turned to thunder. He rose and called out for the attention of those in the room. Andy stepped back and resumed his seat beside Bill, a confused expression on his face after unwittingly arousing the inspector's ire.

"We have a rumor circulation about the recent murder in our village," Jamieson said evenly, "and the manner o' the man's death. Ye can put away all yer thoughts o' brandished swords and decapitation. If ye must know, the victim was stabbed in the chest and a sgian-dubh he wore on his person is missing. Noo, I hope that clears up any misconceptions. And if any o' ye saw anything out of the ordinary last night in the neighborhood o' Crannog Lane, I'd appreciate a chat with ye."

He sat back down and as he did, the group of club's members began to rise and shuffle toward the exit, probably highly stressed by our continued presence at the pub. We'd put a damper on the meeting. They hadn't even ordered. Dallas, Derrick, and Dr. Teague mumbled farewells as they made their way past us. Morag and Brenda paused to speak with Bill and Andy. It appeared that Brenda was introducing them, because I caught the tail-end of her remark. "…and Bill owns the inn next door."

Soon after, Brenda hustled out of the pub without making eye contact. Morag stepped over though and addressed me, "Have you found my handbag yet? Have you caught that robber?"

"We are following up and will have him in custody soon," I assured her.

She waved a dismissive hand. "Yer hunt for a murderer is going to keep all of ye too busy to bother with smaller fry like a car thief. I'm afraid he'll continue tae terrorize the community."

"Officer Stevens is devoting his time to solving the crime."

"Have ye considered that the two crimes could be related? But o' course, ye have."

"We consider everything," Jamieson replied.

"I'm on holiday in Glenkillen," Morag continued. "After hearing how quaint the village was, I booked long in advance. But let me tell you that I am *not* impressed with the latest crime sprees. Robbers, murderers running amok. I'm afraid tae leave my room!"

The inspector interjected. "Until now the village has had very little crime. We'll get tae the bottom o' it and life in Glenkillen will return tae normal."

We watched her leave and the inspector said, "Fer such a fearful woman, she managed tae get herself down here fer a bit o' muckraking."

"FOMO," I said and seeing his questioning expression added, "Fear of missing out."

"So ye would have accepted their invitation."

"Without a second thought," I told him. Then, remembering Ami's text, "By the way, I think I should carry handcuffs."

Jamieson appeared to be thinking it over. Finally, he said, "Aye, with the scrapes ye get yerself into, ye might find them useful."

"*Used* to get myself into," I corrected him. "Past tense."

The inspector raised an eyebrow in reply.

Chapter 7

The middle of the afternoon found us crowded at the kitchen table in my cottage, comparing notes with Vicki and Sean on the members in attendance at the fateful supper. I'd lived in Glenkillen less than a year, so the club members' backgrounds weren't familiar to me. I wasn't sure that the locals in this room would bring much to the table, either, based on a few of my own observations.

Sean was pretty much clueless about interpersonal relationships and showed little interest in small talk with villagers. He had enough trouble opening his ears and really listening when the situation involved a person-of-interest.

The inspector didn't go out of his way to socialize, and his choice to live remotely didn't encourage neighborly meetings on the streets.

Besides, he had neither the time nor the inclination to mingle.

Vicki's younger years were spent in the area, but she'd attained adulthood in the states, and had only returned recently. But she'd picked up enough information to get us started.

"The Irving's have been a fixture in Glenkillen for decades," Vicki informed us while pouring coffee from a carafe she'd brought from the main house. "Dallas' mother ran the bookshop until she retirement, turning it over to Dallas, who'd worked there since she was a kid. Then the mother moved to Inverness into a pensioner's home. Dallas never married, although she's had several long-term relationships, as the rumors go. These days, she shares the apartment above the shop with multiple cats."

My own feline housemate, Snookie, brushed up against my leg, purring. Jamieson peered at her, curiously, as though he'd never seen a cat before. "Stuart spent time at the bookshop," I said. "How close were the two of them?"

Vicki sat down. "I have no idea."

The inspector interjected. "That was one o' my questions tae her. She says he was a regular

73

customer, browsing more than buying, and occasionally requested readings and such. Dallas didn't mind since the events brought in customers. Their relationship was, as she put it, formally friendly."

Vicki nodded. "Dallas is a business owner and because of that she's cordial with everyone."

Which brought us to Morag Lisle, Dallas' last-minute guest.

"I did a wee bit o' lookin' intae her situation," Sean said.

"Ye were supposed tae be hunting fer a robber," the inspector pointed out, his tone lighter than his usual confrontational one with his officer.

Sean hesitated then plunged on. "It was in that line o' inquiry. Up and down Laurel Crescent I went, poundin' on doors, asking questions. Nobody saw the robbery, but the woman renting a room tae her says she's only arrived from Edinburgh, something aboot a divorce and needing time tae herself. Friendly enough, always talking books, even had mentioned the supper and seemed excited."

"That fits with the Morag I met," I said. "Plus, she has a solid alibi, poor woman. She's a visitor on vacation plunged into the thick of things. What about Derrick and Brenda Findlay, Inspector?"

He rearranged his leg, which was perched on a lawn chair that Sean had brought in from outside. He adjusted the icepack I'd insisted that he place on his ankle. "Alibiing each other, they are."

"Wouldn't be the first time a spouse covered fer the other," Sean acknowledged.

My thought exactly. Either trouble had found him outside where he was in the wrong place at the wrong time, a theory we'd all but dismissed, or someone from the group had killed him. Emotions had been running high at the supper table. Even as an observing guest, I'd felt anxious and uncomfortable. The married couple might be protecting one another for a reason.

I remembered information the doctor had supplied. "Dr. Teague told us that Derrick had warned Stuart about his behavior on a prior occasion. And he'd asked Stuart to stay behind after the supper. He could have asked Stuart to leave the club."

"And it would have been about time," Vicki exclaimed. "Stuart brought bad karma to the meetings."

"Did Derrick throw him out then?" Sean said to Jamieson. "Did Findlay tell ye about it during questioning?"

"He didn't mention anything about that when we questioned him after the murder. In fact, he went on about how fine Stuart's reading o' Scott's work had been, and what a tragedy his death would be fer the community."

Snookie chose that moment to leap into Jamieson's lap. I expected him to promptly deposit the cat back on the floor. Instead, to my surprise, he began stroking her. She settled, closed her eyes, and began purring. The inspector was turning out to be a complicated man. Tough one minute, cuddling a cat the next.

I stared at his hand as he continued to pet Snookie. Something about them brought back the dream. What was it about hands?

"How do the Findlay's make a living?" Vicki asked, bringing my attention back to the moment. "They have a lovely place."

Jamieson responded, "A small accounting service out o' their home, taxes and such."

Vicki seemed to be wondering out loud, "If Derrick informed Stuart that he was no longer welcome, imagine how he might have reacted."

"Based on his behavior at the table, not well," I guessed, remembering how quickly the situation had escalated. "He brandished that knife, upsetting both of the Findlays, then he made a veiled threat to Dr. Teague."

Jamieson had been displaying signs of restlessness, shifting in his chair, toying with the ice pack. "Officer Stevens," he said, grabbing the crutches and rising, "find out as much as ye can about Stuart McKay. We already found next o' kin, a sister living in Sterling, and I've spoken with her, broke the bad news. Nothing tae help us on that front. They spoke several times every year, but not recently, and she didn't have any idea as tae who might have wanted to murder her brother.

"Concentrate on his retirement, then on his move tae Glenkillen. If there is a connection between him and anyone at that supper other than through the club, find it!"

Sean was making notes as the inspector turned and spoke to me, the crutches secured under his arms, "Constable Elliott, we need tae pay a visit tae the Findlays."

"Of course."

"Oh, and Stevens, hand over yer handcuffs tae our special constable. Ye can stop at the station and get yerself another pair."

"Yer giving her handcuffs?"

"Aye."

"Well, look at yerself," Sean said to me, handing his over. "Yer almost a proper cop. All ye need is a baton to make it official."

I laughed. "No baton for me. I'll call you if I need that kind of backup."

Outside, driving away, the inspector said, "There. Are ye happy? I gave the lad an important task."

I smiled. "You already researched Stuart's background thoroughly, didn't you?"

That drew a chuckle. "Yer ontae me again."

"You're becoming predictable."

On the way, after calling and confirming that the Findlays were home and willing to speak with us, he filled me in on Stuart's past. "McKay appeared tae be a difficult man tae live with. Three ex-wives, all in

Edinburgh, several grown children scattered here and there."

"Any of them near here?"

"No, and none o' the family interested in chumming with dear old dad. While ye were getting yer beauty sleep this morning, I spoke with the exes and his offspring. No love lost, but no big life insurance payouts tae fight over either. If one o' the exes had murder on her mind, she most likely would o' taken care o' him earlier on. Each o' them claims tae have those who can vouch fer them, and Officer Steven's next project will be confirming alibies. That is, if the lad manages tae report accurately on the information I've already gathered."

"You're testing him?"

"Aye, as tae McKay's career before he retired three years ago and moved tae Glenkillen, McKay was a professor o' Scottish history in Edinburgh. He didn't exactly distinguish himself, but he retired in good graces."

"Morag is from Edinburgh," I pointed out.

"It's a big city. Practically everyone who comes tae visit or stay is from Edinburgh or Glasgow, escaping the big cities."

We stepped out of the car on the street below the Findlay home. My eyes involuntarily landed on the spot where Stuart's body had been found, at the very bottom of the path leading to the house belonging to Brenda and Derrick. A large elm beside the curb that I'd barely noticed the night before would have shielded the attack from view on the dead-end side of the lane. But the side where the taxi driver had spotted the body was exposed. Gone was the tent, the remains, forensic specialist and police, but the street had a grim, tragic feel to it.

I followed the inspector, noting that he was getting better at maneuvering on the crutches.

Inside the Findlay's living room, Derrick gestured for us to sit on a tan leather sofa, and he and Brenda positioned themselves in matching armchairs facing us. After a few forced pleasantries, including questions regarding Jamieson's injury, which he briskly brushed off, the inspector came to the point. "Our job is tae establish the innocence o' as many o' you as possible and tae that end, we have a few more questions regarding the night o' the murder."

"We will help in any way we can." Brenda reached over to the arm of the other chair and patted her husband's hand. "We have nothing tae hide."

"Very well. Ye said Stuart left approximately at ten o'clock."

"That's about right, yes." Brenda removed her hand and folded both of them in her lap. "I still can't believe this happened. That someone attacked Stuart the moment he left our home."

"I hold myself somewhat responsible fer not walking him out," Derrick said. "I might have prevented his death."

"Ye can't blame yerself," his wife said mournfully. "Why, ye might both be dead if ye had."

The inspector steered them back to his own agenda, "What was his mood when he left? I didn't think tae ask ye earlier."

"His mood?" Brenda said, pausing to consider. "Perfectly fine." Then she looked to her husband. "Derrick, don't ye agree?"

Derrick nodded vigorously. "He'd gotten the best of the doctor and seemed delighted with that. And he performed brilliantly fer those of us at the table after enjoying a good meal and a nightcap. As fit as a butcher's dog, I'd say."

"Yet ye'd just informed him that he was no longer welcome at the Scott Suppers?"

The inspector was fishing, of course, hoping to land the truth. But he *did* sound convincing, as though he knew that for a fact.

Derrick seemed to take the question in stride. "But ye see, I didn't. After his aggressive manner toward Dr. Teague, we thought it best tae try a different approach tae the issue at another time."

"Aye," Brenda agreed. "The gathering was filled with enough tension without creating any more. Really, Derrick regretted the invitation tae him tae stay fer a nightcap. We'd had enough of Stuart fer one evening, so we sent him on his way as quickly as we could."

"We dislike speaking ill of the dead," Derrick added.

"He practically threatened the doctor with his knife," I spoke up for the first time. "Over something as simple as a literary disagreement. I can understand your concern for your safety."

"Thank you," Brenda said with relief. "We were afraid tae tell ye about our decision tae remove him in case ye thought Derrick had murdered him. We should have known it would come out and should have been more forthcoming from the beginning."

"Derrick," I pressed on, "did you have the authority to remove Stuart? After all, Dallas is the president."

The inspector's eyes met mine. Was that a glimmer of respect in those piercing blues? Had I just asked a question he hadn't thought of?

Derrick raised his chin. "As vice president, I felt perfectly justified. I tried to discuss it with Dallas after the prior meeting, and she wouldn't even consider it. I decided it was best to proceed without consulting her. I'd confided in the doctor and had his support. It's a moot point anyway, since it didn't happen and now Stuart is dead."

Brenda stood up, signaling the end of our conversation. "Like we said, we were together cleaning up the dishes when we heard a commotion outside. By then it was too late. He had been found and the police called."

"And you didn't hear anything unusual right after he left?" I continued since the inspector seemed content to let me lead. "No raised voices? Screams? Anything?"

"Nothing."

"Do you have your own theory?"

"We have two ideas," Brenda answered. "But you've probably already thought of them."

"Tell us."

"It could have been a random attack by that robber, and Stuart put up a fight where those female pensioners didn't have the strength tae resist, and he was stabbed tae death fer his trouble. Or…" Brenda hesitated.

"Or…," I prompted.

Brenda glanced at Derrick. "Or he'd pushed Dr. Teague too far, and the doctor killed him in a fit of rage."

Derrick nodded along, indicating that the couple had discussed and agreed on their shared opinions.

Later, on the road to the inspector's home to meet Sean for a ride home, Jamieson said, "Derrick and Brenda Findlay are one mind in two bodies."

"Talk about bonded in holy matrimony," I agreed.

If either of them had murdered Stuart, the other might have helped cover it up, the couple united in their shared belief that Stuart McKay had been ultimately responsible for his own demise.

Stuart never should have waved a weapon around at the private gathering. It very well could have been the catalyst for his death.

I still couldn't believe that the village doctor had picked up a knife and used it to harm another human being. I wanted other suspects, someone else to have committed the murder.

And the Findlays were as likely as Teague.

Chapter 8

The hike from my cottage to the moors behind and beyond the farm helped to relieve the stress I carried with me from what had been a very difficult day. Purple heather painted the landscape as far as the eye could see, and its sweet scent drifted up from the sprawling carpet. I heard the hum of busy bees, gathering the heather's sweet nectar while I stood looking at the sweeping valley below and rugged mountains to the north. I remained entranced, feeling the wind in my hair, for an indeterminate period of time before I turned to retrace my steps.

Only then did I notice a man with a familiar gait approaching, a sheepdog at his side.

"There's a Heilan coo over the ridge," Leith said, stopping beside me. He wore well-worn jeans, hiking boots, and a lazy, carefree grin. "I've made friends with that one. Come on, let me show you."

Heilan coos, also known as Highland cows, reminded me of teddy bears with their wavy wooly coats. I broke out in a wide smile at the opportunity to see one close up.

Leith was as handsome as ever, with his sandy blond hair and deep tan from hours spent in his boat on the sea. I couldn't help admiring his physique; this male that kept my fictional hero in sharp focus. "You're in from fishing before dark," I noted, rather surprised to see him. And rather pleased, too. Leith's casual manner always put me at ease.

"Aye, a storm is brewing on the sea."

I crouched to pet Kelly, her tail wagging like mad. She's twelve years old, suffers from arthritis, and cataracts impair her vision. But she's the grande dame of these moorlands, having produced many of the young, talented herding dogs that work the hills today.

We walked over the ridge Leith indicated to find a brindled cow, with long curving horns. It stood perfectly still, staring at us, not twenty yards away.

"A bonnie sight," Leith said after reminding Kelly to stay at his side with a hand motion, her cue to refrain from engaging her herding instincts. "'Tis breeding season, and she's going tae do her part soon enough to grow the fold."

"She?" I wasn't going to attempt to peek under all that thick wool for a gender assessment.

"The horns are the clue," he informed me with a twinkle in his eye. "The male's curve forward and are thicker. This one's curve up. That's the difference." He dug two cookies from a pocket in his fleece. "Let's see if she's hungry fer a ginger cookie."

I retreated a few steps. "I'm not going anywhere near those horns. Besides, she must weigh a thousand pounds!"

Leith laughed. "Our coos are the friendliest in the world and very inquisitive. See, here she comes."

Sure enough, the beast lumbered toward us.

Leith had that big, teasing grin on his face as he strutted to meet her. I tagged along behind him, careful to keep his body between me and the massive beast. "Come on, take the bull by the horns," he quipped, grabbing my arm and trying to pull me forward. "Or in this case, the cow. Here." He thrust a cookie into my hand. "You go first."

"No way." I pulled back. "You do it."

He shook his head in mock disbelief at my cowardliness then focused on his hairy friend. She took the offered cookie gently and munched. "Your turn and give her a little pat or two while yer at it."

Since Leith's fingers were still attached to his hand, and he hadn't been trampled to a bloody pulp, I mimicked his moves, offered the cookie as he had, and watched her chew it. I even rubbed her nose and pushed back her flowing wool to gaze into her eyes. "She's so cute."

"Aye. But we better head back." Leith was studying the sky. "Those storm clouds are moving in fast."

In the distance, lightening flashed. Kelly, sensing our decision, trotted slightly ahead as we returned to the farm. Vicki and Sean peeked out the window at the main house as we passed. Vicki gave a wave and what I thought was a wink as the sky above opened and rain began to fall. We ran past Leith's Land Rover and made it inside with not a moment to spare before the deluge.

Snookie greeted Kelly, going nose to nose, a routine they'd established the day they met. First the noses sniffed cautiously, then a tail wag from one, a light purr from the other.

"It worked out fer the best then?" Leith said, referring to my initial reluctance to adopt the Scottish fold.

"I couldn't imagine my life without her," I answered, realizing the truth of it as I took a seat in one of two armchairs beside the wood burning stove in the corner. Leith started a fire and joined me while Kelly stretched out to enjoy the warmth and Snookie watched from a perch on the end table.

"I hear that the village is goin' through a rough patch," he said. "And yer in the thick of it again."

I nodded. "Not only is a car thief terrorizing the community, but Stuart McKay was murdered right after a supper I attended."

I went on to relate details of the Scott Supper and its aftermath. "The inspector wants us to focus our efforts on the club members." I couldn't tell him that Dr. Teague was the frontrunning suspect since I was part of the investigation and privy to information not available to others. Leith and even Vicki had to remain outside the loop.

"It's good that ye and Vicki have solid alibis," Leith said. "Having Sean to vouch fer the two o' you is good fortune. Ye can check off Dallas Irving as well. She wouldn't do a thing like that. The others I know little about."

"You know the doc."

"Never been tae his surgery." Leith grinned. "I'm as fit as a fiddle."

The fire crackled. The heat radiating outward into the room warmed me. "What brought you to the moor?" I asked him after a comfortable silence.

Leith slouched back in the chair and gazed at me. "I knocked at yer cottage. When ye didn't answer, I inquired at the main house. Vicki pointed me in yer direction, saying ye needed cheering up after chasing a killer all day. She's playin' Cupid, I do believe, based on her sly manner. And Sean is right with her."

I tried not to blush and most likely failed. It had been obvious to me that they were trying to set us up, but if Leith figured it out, did everyone know?

"I've noticed," I admitted. "They are engaged to be married and still in that blissful state, and assuming I need the same thing. Two good-intentioned busybodies."

"And do ye?"

"Do I what?"

"Need the same thing?"

Ah, that was the big question I'd been wrestling with. Did I need a man to feel complete? I'd had one in the past and look how that had turned out. Instead of the two of us becoming soulmates, I'd crawled away broken into pieces, my soul barely intact.

"Are *you* looking for what Vicki and Sean have?" I dodged and countered.

"We aren't talkin' about me, Eden Elliott." He rose, hands on hips and smiled. "But never mind answering, if it doesn't suit ye."

It didn't suit me. This was too awkward. Leith has been my friend since the first day I arrived, but until now we'd only shared friendly, casual banter. Nothing more. Now, although he was smiling, I sensed a serious undertone.

Lightening flashed close by, followed by a clap of thunder, giving me a few minutes to gather my thoughts. "The answer is no. I don't need what they have, if it means settling. But someday I want it. And what about you?"

Leith walked to the window and peered out. Then he answered slowly. "Ye know I had a bad experience with Fia's mum, and after we split, I vowed tae myself tae leave romance alone and concentrate on raising my daughter."

I understood. He'd mentioned his commitment to his daughter before. At the time, it seemed noble. Now, I thought it restricted him to a very lonely life. Especially during those times when Fia was with her mother.

He turned from the window. "My lifestyle isn't suited fer a companion. I'm out tae sea more than on land and it isn't fair tae have someone waiting at home and wondering if I'll make it back."

I could have said that I wasn't like most women, that I needed personal space, that while married to a controlling, demanding man, I'd nearly suffocated to death. Having a partner who would come and go and come back again would be as refreshing as a sea breeze.

I gazed at the flames in the fire, thinking about Leith's life and coming to the realization that the man really wasn't lonely. He was a loner. He kept his circle small by choice, preferring spending time with his daughter when he could and out on the waves for the rest. Perhaps his ex-wife had needed more companionship and had been the lonely one in that relationship.

"Let the tongues wag," I told him. "I'm not concerned with gossip."

"If I stay any longer, they'll be jabbering all over the village and we won't have a moment's peace. I'll say my farewell. Rest well."

After Leith and Kelly left, I sat by the fire, wondering about my future, reminding myself to enjoy the present. In spite of murderous undertones in Glenkillen, my life was fulfilling and perfect as it was. For now, anyway.

That night, with the storm raging, my faceless lover didn't make the customary appearance in my dreams. I suspected that my subconscious knew my heart and was waiting for my conscious mind to catch up.

Chapter 9

"Did you have breakfast this morning?" I asked the inspector, who was scowling at us from his easy chair, first boring holes in me with his piercing eyes, then Sean, then repeating the snarly process. We'd arrived together and on time, and Jamieson's unprovoked, uncalled for negative attitude wasn't brightening this drizzly day.

"Well, did you?" I stood before him, tote on my shoulder, hands on hips, determined not to back down.

"What's that got tae do with anything?"

"He doesn't take breakfast," Sean answered for him.

The inspector raised his hands in an expression of irritation. "And I thought I was in the room and well able tae answer fer myself."

"You weren't going to answer," I pointed out, heading for the kitchen.

"And what do ye think yer doing?"

"Making your breakfast," I called over my shoulder. "And if you don't eat it, I'm not driving you anywhere."

Silence ensued while I found a toaster and popped two slices of bread in, which I'd packed in the tote along with peanut butter and Dundee orange marmalade. While I waited for the bread to brown, I opened the refrigerator and several cupboards, taking an assessment, wondering how the man existed without pantry essentials and with a bare refrigerator. Once the bread was crisp and brown, I slathered on the spreads.

My return earned me a scoff when I forced him to take the plate. "Eat," I demanded.

"Yer a hard woman."

"Consider this a health-related experiment." One I hoped would work. Since yesterday, when I'd seen him revert back to a normal human being after a bowl of soup, I began to suspect that he had a low blood sugar problem. That would explain his early day grumpiness.

Sean took the floor while the inspector grudgingly bit into the toast. The younger officer reiterated exactly what Jamieson had learned the day before, passing the test that the inspector had devised: a sister in Oban, three former wives, grown children, Stuart's career as a history professor.

Jamieson gaped at Sean.

"Good work," I exclaimed.

"Aye," the inspector stammered. "Wonders never cease."

"And I'm drivin' tae Edinburgh after lunch tae check out the wifies' alibis." Sean looked sheepish. "I mean, if that's what will progress the case and ye approve it."

Jamieson was trying to hold back a chuckle, confirming two facts for me. One: his upward mood reversal immediately after eating suggested I'd been right. Two: he was slowly and reluctantly beginning to trust in Sean's abilities.

"That's exactly what I was about tae order ye tae do!" Jamieson said with a bit of wonder in his voice. "We'll make a detective out o' ye yet. Noo, what about any connection with the other club members? Anything from the victim's past that intersects with any o' them?"

Sean shook his head. "I'll keep digging. But I can't get rid of the notion that this crime might o' been random. I still think that our victim might have seen something that got him killed."

The inspector finished eating and shook his head. "And what was this something? Nobody has reported a crime in the area. I have footage fer the two o' ye tae watch, if one o' you will fetch my laptop."

I did the honors and soon we were looking at surveillance video footage. "On the street in front of the Findlays." I recognized the setting.

"Watch."

Stuart appeared in profile on the very perimeter of the video. He paused on the sidewalk and swung his head to the side as though he was aware of someone approaching. Then he stepped out of the frame into the shadows as though he'd been called over.

"That's all we have?" Sean said with disappointment.

"He's calm and relaxed," I noted. "And appears to be joining someone. By his body language, I think he knew his killer."

"And that person had the smarts tae stay out of the camera's range," the inspector added.

"Nothing random about this. Now let's get tae work."

Sean drove off as Jamieson moved to his police car, more confident and balanced on the crutches. He ducked inside after I opened the door for him. "As I stated tae ye before, I'm not satisfied tae follow a theory that the murder was random or that the car thief was involved," he said. "In that spirit, I asked myself who else might o' known about the Scott Supper and that McKay would be in attendance."

I closed his door, went around, and climbed into the driver's seat. "Don't we have enough suspects already?"

"Ye'd like it tae be that simple, and sure it might be. I questioned Brenda Findlay. She's active on social media, addicted tae it, if ye ask me. She posted a photo of the last supper with names and the date o' this one fer the whole world tae know. Anyone with an axe tae grind with the professor would have known where tae find him."

"That's a discouraging thought," I said with dismay. The investigation was difficult enough with only a handful of suspects. I was overwhelmed by all the possibilities. "And of course, those in attendance probably shared their plans for the evening with others," I added. "I know I did. We couldn't possible track down everyone who knew about the supper."

We'd been sitting stationary while mulling over a list of suspects that covered the globe. "If Dr. Teague was the person in the shadows, wouldn't Stuart have reacted strongly to his adversary's presence in the dark?"

"One would think."

"By the way, where are we heading?"

"Let's pay another call tae Teague, exert a wee bit o' pressure."

*

We found the doctor tending his plants in a walled garden behind the surgery. Bluebells and daffodils framed the gate as we stepped inside. Dr. Teague was picking stalks of rhubarb from a well-established, large-leaved plant. He straightened and removed the gardening gloves he wore.

"I don't have long," he said, tossing the gloves on the path beside a small garden shed. "My first patient arrives in ten minutes. How's yer ankle?"

"Better. I'm tossing the crutches soon. They're awkward tae use and slow me down." Jamieson leaned against the shed. "But let's not use up the few minutes ye have talking about me. It's a fact among the club members that the animosity between McKay and yerself began before the night in question. Ye need tae do a more thorough job o' explaining yer relationship with the victim then ye did yesterday."

The doc picked up a paring knife and began to trim the rhubarb stalks he'd cut. "There's nothing more tae explain. I rubbed him the wrong way."

"You appeared to be giving as much as you got," I interjected. "The situation escalated because you pushed his buttons."

The doctor paused in his task and glanced at me. "Perhaps I *did* contribute to the situation. The man was a pompous bore!"

"Now that's the honesty we need from ye," Jamieson said. He'd been checking his cell phone and placed it on the shed's window sill. "However, ye deal with difficult patients all the time and don't jump intae going head tae head with them. Ye practice patience and hold yer tongue in the profession ye chose, isn't that right?"

"Stuart McKay wasn't one of my patients."

"And why not?" the inspector asked. "Aren't ye the only doctor in Glenkillen? Surely, he's been in tae see ye?"

"Like I said, he wasn't a patient." Teague glanced at his watch. "We'll have to continue this conversation another time."

"We will indeed," Jamieson replied.

Back on the sidewalk in front of the surgery, we were about to leave when a middle-aged woman in a ratty bathrobe and fluffy slippers hurried our way and stopped a few yards away.

"Psst," she said to get our attention, although she already had mine. She motioned us toward her. "I don't want tae be seen by the doctor. Is he in the window? Act like nothin's amiss."

Jamieson swung toward her and I followed, passing in front of the surgery window.

"Around the corner, if ye please," the woman said, moving along ahead of us.

Once she was satisfied with our distance from the surgery, she addressed me in a stage whisper, "I heard about the murder, and I have information ye might find useful, if ye know what I mean."

I glanced at the inspector, suppressing a show of excitement. Was this the break we needed?

She continued talking to me as though the inspector didn't exist. "I saw ye here before, and here ye are again today. It got me thinking that ye must have something on the doctor. Did he kill Stuart McKay?"

"We're still in the early stages of the investigation," I said, careful not to rush her, but really wanting her to get to the point.

"And we don't discuss details during it," Jamieson added. "What's yer name and what's this information ye want tae report?"

The woman glanced at him, then up and down the street as though she were part of a clandestine operation. "Poppy Smith, I am, and I was in the surgery when Stuart came in and made a scene, late February or early March, I can't be sure, but it was around that time."

"What kind of scene?" I asked.

"The whole waiting room was full, everybody having bad colds from what was going around, including meself. He walked right in, waited fer the doctor tae call the next patient. When that came about, he insisted that he be taken intae the exam room next. The doc refused and Stuart McKay got riled and called him a quack and a fraud right tae his face. The doctor threatened tae call the police if he didn't leave and so he did, lookin' all satisfied with himself. And why would he say a thing like that? Dr. Teague is one o' the best doctors tae hang a shingle in Glenkillen. Not that Doc Keen wasn't good in his time, but he should o' retired years ago."

The inspector asked her several more questions but uncovered nothing else worthwhile. We thanked her for stepping forward and watched her until she walked up onto a porch and into a house down the street.

"I understand why the doctor might be reluctant to mention that particular incident," I said. "Not only would it have been embarrassing to be called out like that in front of his patients, but it gives him another excellent reason for disliking Stuart. It would have been better to hear it from him rather than one of his patients."

"It must o' conveniently slipped his mind." Jamieson began patting pockets the way we do when we are missing something on our person. "I must o' left my mobile in the garden."

"You placed it on the window sill during the conversation. It must still be there. I'll get it for you."

He waited beside the car while I followed the path back into the garden. His phone was where he'd left it on the window sill.

I reached to pick it up and, as I did, my eye caught color on the sill to the left of the phone. Looking closely, I recognized the stain for what it surely must be.

Blood.

Chapter 10

We entered the surgery and waited impatiently for Dr. Teague to finish up with his patient. As luck would have it, no one else was in the waiting room when the inspector asked for permission to search the premises.

"Yer interest in me is bordering on harassment," the doctor said, sounding annoyed. "Are ye searching the private homes of all the attendees from the Scott Supper?"

"Is that an aye tae the search?"

"Absolutely bloody not! And I'm asking ye tae leave right now!"

After our ousting, Jamieson sat in his vehicle while making calls to arrange a warrant. My assigned task was to guard the garden in the off-chance that the doctor made an attempt to enter the garden and tamper with evidence.

Sean called my cell while I waited.

"I've been tasked with delivering the warrant as soon as it's obtained," he said importantly. "Are ye making sure the scene is secure?"

"You don't need to worry about me," I countered. "Just get your own job done."

"Well, aren't we snippy."

I hung up rather abruptly and evaluated my current emotional state. Yes, snippy and jumpy. Anxious and worried. Dreading the possibility of a scene and preparing a response if the doctor appeared ahead of Jamieson and confronted me. My eyes darted to a rear window where the doctor could easily be watching.

I peered through the shed window, as I'd done after finding the smudge of blood. At least there hadn't been a dead body or injured person inside. That much I'd confirmed before reporting to the inspector. What then? Why the blood?

The explanation might be as simple as a small cut to the doctor's finger while trimming. Accidentally drawing blood while working in a garden wasn't that unusual, considering the array of tools used and the sharpness of some of them.

The inspector was an opportunist by nature and career, and he'd pounced on this advantage like a tiger on its prey. Evidence had been stacking up against the doctor; the blood presented a perfect chance to search his property.

It seemed like forever before Jamieson finally rounded the corner of the building, sans crutches but sporting a noticeable limp. Dr. Teague followed, and Sean had taken up the rear, with what I assumed was the warrant clutched in his hand.

"This is an outrage," the doctor sputtered. "Get yer business done and off my property! Ye have no cause and I can't understand how ye even were able tae obtain a search warrant for my shed!"

"We have tae follow up on every lead," Sean told him. "Stand over there and keep yer thoughts tae yerself while we go about our business. I'll be keeping ye company so don't try any funny business."

Jamieson ignored the two men, handing me a pair of gloves, which I snapped on. Then he motioned me to open the shed door. He followed me inside. Defused light streaked through the window pane. The air smelled earthy. Garden tools hung neatly on hooks, pots were stacked below the window, and a hodgepodge of garden items decorated a worktable. Twine, hand tools, work gloves.

This would be my first time searching a suspect's property, and I planned to leave no stone unturned. We were looking for Stuart's decorative knife—that was clearly presumed. Since the inspector wasn't wearing gloves, it was also safe to assume I was the one who would be conducting the search. Under his watchful eye, of course.

The worktable had three drawers down the left side, and I started by opening the top one. While the rest of the shed appeared tidy, this drawer was jammed with items. But the disorganization wasn't a problem, because the focus of our search was right on top in the very first drawer. That was all it took. Less than a minute.

"Well, what da ye know." The inspector voice was clear and cold. "A sgian-dubh in the most unlikely o' places." He held open a clear bag. "Pick it up without maulin' the thing, use the paper underneath it and remove both. That's it. Now carefully drop them in this bag."

"I hate this," I said, let down by our finding, disappointed in the medical doctor.

"Let's go break it tae Teague."

The doctor's behavior when we confronted him struck me as characteristic of any accused man, predictable for an accused suspect whether that person was guilt or not. He paled when he saw the knife. Then he denied any knowledge of the ownership or reason for its appearance among his belongings. "Never had one, never borrowed one, and this certainly isn't mine." Then his expression shifted to angry. "Did ye set me up? Plant it?" He glared at me. "Or did he?"

I hadn't predicted this reaction.

Jamieson stayed cooler than I did, although I witnessed a small tick in his jaw.

"You can't be serious!" I exclaimed. "You're accusing us of planting evidence in your shed?" My voice hit a high note. "Of all the crazy…"

"We'll be taking ye in fer questioning," the inspector interrupted, addressing the doctor while I yanked off the gloves. "Ye best lock up the surgery fer the rest o' the day. And ye can forget that cockamamie idea about us planting anything. Ye've been watching too many American crime shows."

A few minutes later, I stood on the curb, unsure of my role since the inspector had abandoned his crutches. Was I driving? Riding shotgun? What?

"Ye best be off to Edinburgh," the inspector said to Sean once he'd deposited the doctor in the back of his police car.

"No need now," Sean informed him. "Ye have yer killer. The wifies are in the clear."

The inspector jerked open the driver's door. "I could put ye on traffic control in the village center, if ye don't like this particular task."

"I best be off then."

"And take Eden…eh…Constable Elliott home tae get her vehicle. I'm through needing a chauffeur in spite o' her capable driving skills."

Under different circumstances, I would have been pleased by that remark, recalling what a disaster I'd been behind the wheel in the first months. Driving on the left side of the road and entering roundabouts in the opposite direction had been challenging.

Sean was quiet on the way back to the farm, allowing me time to process the most recent finding. My gut feeling had been that the doctor was innocent. Yet, he had means, considering the knife found in his possession. And motive, after Stuart had disparaged him in front of patients and had publicly threatened him. And plenty of opportunity to commit the murder since he didn't have anyone to confirm that he'd been anywhere other than in the shadows at Crannog Lane.

So why was the inspector sending Sean to confirm other alibis, if he thought the case was airtight? Was Sean's daytrip to Edinburgh nothing other than a merry chase to keep the new officer out of his hair? Or was he unsure about Teague's guilt and wanted to continue to investigate other possibilities?

From past cases, I knew that Dr. Teague could be held for at least twenty-four hours. Jamieson would use every minute of that time to try to further prove his guilt or his innocence. Then, he would have to let him go or charge him with murder.

There were still a few questions that seemed to conflict with the evidence. For example, why would the doctor goad Stuart at a private party in front of witnesses if he intended to murder him a few hours later? And why would he stash the murder weapon inside his own shed, in a drawer, right on top where it couldn't be missed? I also needed to know whose blood I had found on the window sill and why it was in that particular spot.

Teague's accusation against us played in my head again. He'd wanted to know if we'd planted the weapon—if we were setting him up?

That was absurd.

But I sensed that perhaps someone else was.

And I wasn't about to let the doctor go down for the crime, if he didn't do it. And I believed that was what the inspector demanded as well. But at the moment, Dr. Teague was the only one at the Scott Supper with a motive for killing Stuart McKay.

I could let it unravel naturally, let it work itself out under the guidance of Jamieson. But the inspector had doubts, too, I was sure of it, and I thought I detected his consent for further investigation when he ordered Sean to Edinburgh. I decided to be aggressive rather than passive, to arrange a gathering of my own at the Kilt & Thistle.

And this time it would be all-inclusive.

Chapter 11

We met in the early afternoon at the same table that Dallas, Brenda, Derrick, Morag, and the late-arriving doctor had occupied yesterday. This time, I maneuvered into the head position at the table with Vicki seated at my side. Whether or not I had the legal right to interrogate the group as a volunteer constable was a question for which I conveniently didn't pursue an answer.

As to the inspector, I'd failed to notify him in case he wouldn't view my plan in a positive light.

Everyone had agreed to the meeting. FOMO, I imagined.

After we'd ordered beverages and exchanged small talk for a suitable period of time, Dallas inquired about the doctor. "Where is he?"

"Dr. Teague is assisting with the investigation by responding to more inquires," I replied, having anticipated the question and prepared for it.

"I knew it!" Brenda banged an open hand on the table. "He murdered Stuart!"

"That's premature," I answered. "He's simply cooperating with the investigation." There, was that vague enough?

"As we all have," Morag said. "Please let this be done with soon. I've been warned tae remain in the village. I'd like tae be away from here as soon as I'm allowed tae leave. My holiday has turned into a jail sentence."

"It isn't pleasant for any of us to be suspects in a murder investigation," Vicki said politely. "But we must make the most of it. The more we cooperate with the authorities, the sooner this will be over."

"What do ye mean *we?*" Brenda asked Vicki. "Ye make it sound like yer a suspect as well, when we all know that ye and Eden alibied out very nicely, thanks tae that fiancé of yours."

I could have mentioned that she and Derrick had done the same for each other. Instead I tried to appease everyone. "We all want the truth and we want justice for Stuart."

Derrick leaned into the table. "Tae tell ye the truth, nobody especially liked McKay. He was stuck on himself, and had an adversarial disposition."

"Aye," his wife agreed. "He riled all with his harsh words."

Morag leaned in as well, conspiratorially, "I hardly knew the man, but he didn't make a good impression, that's fer sure."

"*Time will rust the sharpest sword,*" Derrick said.

"*Time will consume the strongest cord,*" said his wife.

Morag stared at the couple with a puzzled expression. "What are ye speakin' of?"

"I'm not following, as well," I agreed.

"Quotes from Sir Walter Scott," Dallas informed us. "Classics."

I was still confused by the bookshop owner's explanation. "How does that apply to the murder of Stuart McKay?"

"The quotes are from Harold the Dauntless," Dallas explained. "It was Scott's last long verse narrative and he decided tae publish it anonymously. He was curious tae know if his critics would detect his hand in it." She glanced at Brenda. "Honestly, I don't understand the reference, either."

"Again, what does that have to do with this?" I prompted, addressing the Findlays.

"Ye detected the doctor's hand in this, didn't ye?" Brenda attempted to explain. "A direct stab tae the heart with the skill o' a medical professional and his dislike fer Stuart. He wasn't able tae hide behind anonymity."

I sighed. "The doctor has *not* been charged with any crime." Not yet anyway.

Derrick and Brenda, united and potential co-conspirators, were certainly offhanded when discussing a man who'd been murdered practically on their doorstep. And neither expressed shock at assuming that the doctor had done the deed.

I was about to stir the pot, mix a little confusion in with the brew. "I'd like to suggest another theory; one that you might think is a bit farfetched. But take some time to consider it."

Vicki spoke up on cue. "They might be wondering why they should trust you, Eden, with you being a constable. Or me, for that matter, for being engaged to a police officer."

I studied each of them then said, "Unless you are guilty, you have no reason to distrust me. We are on the same side."

117

"Of course," Morag said, her tone turning friendly. "What's yer theory?"

"Dr. Teague and Stuart McKay have had their differences and on more than one occasion the public was privy to their squabbles. Not only that, the doctor doesn't have a proper alibi," At this I paused momentarily before adding, "and I should point out that some of you at this table don't either, but that doesn't make you a killer."

"Derrick and I were together," Brenda made sure to announce.

I continued on, presenting my hypothesis, "We've all been to the doctor's office for one thing or another. No one had a bad word to say about him, other than Stuart. Before the supper, before some of us became suspects in Stuart's murder, would any of us have thought our local doctor capable of this crime? Especially, considering his chosen field. Surely, he's had to deal with difficult personalities many times over. Are you really going to believe that this time he snapped because the two of them disagreed over national novelists?"

"Yer theory is that the doc didn't do it?" Derrick asked. "That's not much o' a theory, Eden."

"I'm suggesting that the doctor is being framed."

The table went quiet while they took this in, their faces reflecting first surprise then doubt. "It *is* a stretch of the imagination," I admitted. "And it takes a calculating and twisted mind to use an innocent man that way."

"I don't believe any of us are capable of such a thing," Brenda said.

Vicki remained silent beside me, well aware of my intention to cast uncertainty among them. There was little doubt in my mind that either the killer really was the doctor or someone sitting at the table at this very moment had murdered Stuart and had further plotted to turn suspicion on Teague.

"What about his ex-wives?" Dallas asked.

"Stuart's exes and adult children have been interviewed and we are following up on their whereabouts. We haven't eliminated them as suspects, but if my theory is correct, we can conclude that they are the least likely to have been framing Dr. Teague, since they knew nothing of the animosity between Stuart and the doctor."

"That doesn't mean one of them didn't kill him," Derrick said dryly.

"That's true," I agreed. "We're following up on their alibis."

"Yer suggesting one o' us then, according tae yer idea?" Brenda looked suspiciously at the group. "At this very table? One o' us killed Stuart and is attempting to implicate Dr. Teague?"

"I'm only saying it's a possibility."

Morag looked doubtful. "And what reason would any of us have fer doing a thing like that?"

I didn't have an answer for that yet and was relieved when the moment was interrupted by a disturbance at the counter. We turned our attention there.

Bill and Andy Morris had arrived and were standing at the bar. Dale placed two drinks before them while a small elderly woman with bluish gray hair tucked into a bun and sitting on a barstool made a ruckus.

"I tell ye, that's him!" she shouted, pointing at Andy. "He robbed me in my car just the other day!"

Andy's freckled face registered panic. "Yer...yer mistaken, ye are."

She jumped down from the stool, glared up at Andy, who was twice her height, and grabbed him by the arm. Her eyes swung my way.

"Yer a constable, aren't ye?" she called out.

I rose from the table. "Yes."

"Arrest this tosser!"

Andy's eyes met mine and his went as wild as a caged animal. He yanked his arm free, almost toppling the woman and bolted out the door.

I was right behind him.

Why I thought I could catch him was beyond me. Or why I felt a need to try, since I knew who he was and could easily track him down. Andy was half my age. Thirty-eight and counting is no time to take up sprinting without easing into it with a responsible training plan. In a few leaping bounds he had outdistanced me, yet I continued the pursuit.

Past the Whisky Shop and A Taste of Scotland. Next, he veered left, leaving the tourist office in his dust. Then he vanished into the Glenkillen cemetery on the hill.

I paused at the cemetery's gate, scanning the grave stones and trees, finding no sign of Andy. I collapsed on the soft grass at the entryway. Gasping, struggling to fill my lungs with air, I finally found a clear, deep breath.

I sat there for a few minutes recovering before I would return to the pub and interview the blue-haired pensioner.

As luck would *not* have it, Jamieson's police vehicle pulled up beside me. He rolled down the window. "We're in the middle o' a murder investigation and yer lollygaggin'. Getting some fresh air, are ye?"

I covered my face with a hand and rubbed my temple. "I was chasing a suspect."

"It appears that yer target has gotten away from ye." The inspector's shrewd blue eyes took in the quiet cemetery then bore into me. "And what suspect are ye referring tae, may I ask."

"Andy Morris. He's been accused of car robbery."

"Ye better get in and explain yerself. This is turning out tae be quite the day."

Chapter 12

The accusing woman introduced herself as Rhona Selkirk. She recognized the inspector immediately and directed her first question to him. "Inspector, did the girl catch him?"

"Ye can ask her yerself," Jamieson said, leaving me to shake my head in the negative.

"He was fast," was all I had to offer.

The club members had cleared out, but Morag remained behind citing her personal interest in apprehending the robber as her reason. A valid one considering she'd been one of his victims. She sat beside Rhona, two women with a common bond.

"Rhona was confined in her trunk as well," the inspector informed me, and I remembered him describing her as feisty at the time of the incident.

"I could o' caught him a few years back," Rhona announced, looking me up and down and, by her expression, finding me lacking in either stamina

123

or intelligence or perhaps both. "And ye even were wearing trainers," she said, glancing at my feet and shaking her head.

I shrugged. "We know who he is and where he lives. He won't get far. Where's Bill?"

"He left," Morag said. "Right after you went on yer foot chase."

"We know how tae find the uncle, too," the inspector said. "Now, Rhona, tell me what happened in here."

"I came in tae get a nice bowl o' hot soup. A wee bit after I ordered, here comes Bill with that nephew o' his and they order drinks and stand there yammering with each other. All of a sudden, I got a spooked feeling, like I better pay attention. I get them once in a while and they're dead on. I knew he was hairy at the heels the minute I turned and saw him."

"Who might ye be referring tae?" Jamieson asked. "Bill or his nephew?"

"The nephew, that's who. Dodgy looking. Although the other was no prize, either. Anybody ought tae be able tae see he's trouble by the shift in his eyes. He robbed me and he's going tae pay behind bars. And I want my purse back all accounted fer and I want him tae get me a new phone, one o' them fancy ones that cost a lot."

"Are you absolutely sure Andy Morris is the one who robbed you?" I asked. "How can you be so certain? Wasn't the man who attacked you wearing a mask?"

Rhona crossed her arms firmly and tipped her chin. "Young lady," she said. "I could pick him out o' a lineup a mile long. And it wasn't his face that I recognized, although he has a look about him. It was his voice. Everybody's voice is one o' a kind, chust like fingerprints. And that stutter of his was enough tae identify him. I should have hit him with my new purse."

I glanced at a large red handbag next to her on the counter.

"Let's go talk to Bill," Jamieson said to me.

"I'm coming, too," Morag said.

"No," the inspector said. "The two o' ye stay put."

"You did well, ma'am," I said to Rhona.

"Is there a reward?" she asked. "I could use a wee bit extra."

"Justice should be reward enough," said the inspector.

*

Day after day, Jeannie Morris runs the Whistling Inn next door to the pub while Bill wastes his life away drinking. His daughter shows her rebellious side with a nose ring and brash bottled red hair, but she's reliable and runs a successful establishment.

"Ye looking fer my da," she said, wagging her head in the general direction of the dining room. "He's in there." Then she addressed the inspector, "But he says he won't speak tae you. Only her."

"He doesn't have a say," Jamieson said.

"It's all right." I placed a hand on his arm. "I can handle this."

"Fine then. Ye go ahead and talk tae the old bugger."

Bill had poured himself a drink from a wet bar and was waiting for me. "I did everything I could fer that boy," he said. But I knew him as an unreliable narrator. The man could barely take care of himself. "Took him in when his parents didn't know what to do with him. Thought I'd saved him from a life o' crime. Now this. He's made his bed, now he has tae lie in it."

"Where is he?" I demanded.

"Not sure, at the moment. He's been staying upstairs. Room seven. Jeannie can give ye the key."

"For the record, I'm taking that as consent to enter without a warrant." I was already striding toward the front desk, pleased with myself for sounding official.

Rhona Selkirk had been certain of Andy's guilt. And he'd run away when confronted. I agreed with her accounting. Andy was our guy.

We climbed the stairs. I pretended not to notice Jamieson's grunts of discomfort. We entered room number seven.

I didn't locate anything of significance in dresser drawers or under the bed. Any cash that the women carried likely had disappeared into Andy's pocket. The purses he would have disposed of.

"Not so smart, after all," the inspector announced while searching through a backpack tucked in the far corner of the closet. He produced a black ski mask, gloves, and a knife matching the description presented by the women.

On the way out, Jamieson said to Jeannie, "tell him tae turn himself in. He's making his future worse by running."

"I'll do that," she said, glancing at the backpack.

We returned to the pub where Morag and Rhona still sat at the bar, heads together, commiserating.

"Did ye get him?" Rhona asked, this time addressing me.

"Not yet," I answered.

"Shame, a young thing like ye are couldn't o' run him down."

What could I say?

Later in the evening, after Sean returned from Edinburgh with solid alibis for Stuart McKay's ex-wives and adult children, while sitting in Vicki's kitchen with pints of ale in front of us, I wondered out loud what I would have done if I'd caught up with Andy and he'd continued to resist.

After slurping a sip of his beer, Sean said, "I'd have clubbed him with me baton, zapped him with the stun gun, and handcuffed him tae the nearest lamppost."

Vicki chortled, since we both knew Sean better than that.

In hindsight, I could have opened up with pepper spray, if I'd thought to bring it along. Instead, it had been on the seat of my Peugeot, doing no one any good. But it was a moot point. I hadn't been in range to use it anyway.

"Why would Bill's nephew join our community and then rob our residents?" I asked.

"It must be in his nature," Vicki answered. "He had a record before he arrived, and that'll go against him in court." Then she smiled. "Leave it to Rhona to expose him. He messed with the wrong woman."

"She's a fire cracker," I agreed.

A moment later, my cell phone rang. Jeannie Morris was on the other end. "Ye best come. Andy's being held and he's confessed."

"Held? By the inspector?"

"Rhona Selkirk and Morag Lisle have him. They staked out the inn and waited fer him tae show up. Ye better get here before they do something awful tae him."

Sean and I got there as fast as we could and stormed up to room seven where the women had secured Andy to the bedframe with ropes of yarn in a fusion of lullaby hues; pink, baby blue, and soft yellow. A knitting bag lay open on the floor.

"Help!" he shouted when we walked in. "I fear fer...fer my life."

I stifled a grin. Rhona and Morag were practically sitting on him. "Jeannie said you confessed."

"I did it," he cried, and I thought he looked so young and helpless now. "I h...held up grannies in their cars and s...stole from them. But it's not like I s..stole their cars, only a few dollars."

"Who are ye calling a grannie?" Morag snarled.

"Ye took our phones, too," Rhona said.

"That was so ye couldn't sq...squeal on me."

Sean attempted to unknot the yarn around Andy's wrists. "We have yer phones," he told the women. "And Andy is going tae make sure yer reimbursed fer yer losses. And he's going tae jail."

"I had tae ruin the yarn I was working into a blanket fer my new grandbaby." Rhona dug in the knitting bag, found a pair of scissors, and began snipping through the yarn binding Andy. "Ye owe me fer me yarn, too."

"What about Stuart McKay?" Morag ask me. "This bloke might have murdered Stuart!"

"Wha'? No, I d…didn't do that. Am I being charged with that? I d…didn't do anything. I didn't even know the man."

Sean snapped handcuffs around his wrists. "Punks like yerself stick tae petty crimes, I'm betting. But yer on the short list as far as the boss is concerned, that's fer sure."

"I'm filing charges against these two wo…women fer assault," Andy said.

Chapter 13

"You need more excitement in your life," Ami texted next morning while I was enjoying a cup of coffee with Snookie lounging on my lap.

More excitement! She was kidding, right? But then I realized that my stateside friend didn't know the latest turn of events.

"Does tracking a murderer and apprehending a robber count as enough excitement?" I texted back.

"Really? Wow! You should write a book! Oh, wait, you are writing one!"

Not exactly, I might have said, but then I'd get the seat-in-the-chair and hands-on-the-keyboard lecture. Right now, romance and love scenes were on hold, replaced by murder and crime scenes.

However, in my dreams...I'd had that same one again. The bed, the faceless lover, those hands, the rest. I so wanted to tell Ami about it, but sharing would only set her off again.

"Gotta go," I thumbed in after an incoming call was announced.

"Inspector," I said. "Good morning."

"Ye certainly were busy last night," he said without preamble.

"Is this a congratulatory call?"

"If yer lookin' fer a 'well-done', that honor is reserved fer Rhona and Morag."

"They restrained him with knitting yarn." I grinned at the memory of Andy tied to the bed. "We're making progress," I said, turning serious. "One criminal down, one to go. Did you question Andy about the murder?"

"Jeannie confirmed his whereabouts at the time."

I sighed. "Another family member vouching for a suspect."

"Andy wasn't even bright enough tae hide his knife and mask well. Leaving them in his closet proves he isn't a brain trust. The galoot doesn't have it in him tae get away with murder."

"And the doctor?"

"Teague hasn't confessed, but the evidence against him is pretty solid. No prints on the knife, however. Anybody could o' placed it in the shed. And not a single eyewitness tae the murder."

"What about the blood on the shed's window sill?"

"Pig's blood. The supermarkets carry it fer making black pudding. As ye know, it's easy tae come by." I did know that, based on another killer's ruse that I'd been involved with.

"Blood might have been smeared there in hopes of drawing us into the shed and to the knife discovery," I said.

"Aye, It's highly possible, but pure speculation at this stage."

"If so, someone is going to a lot of trouble to implicate the doctor."

"No fingerprints on the knife tae make our job easy, either. I'm going over tae speak with Derrick and Brenda Findlay again. They were the last tae see the victim alive. Officer Stevens will follow up with Dallas Irving and Morag Lisle. And I'm going tae have a chat with Andy Morris. Do ye want tae join me?"

As much as I wanted to hear what Andy had to say, I'd chosen another mission for this morning. "I have a few ideas I'd like to chase down."

After that, I showered, dressed in jeans and pulled a fleece over my t-shirt, and headed out in the Peugeot, my thoughts whirling with all the possibilities, the vast array of outcomes. I found myself vacillating where the doctor was concerned, when at other times I'd seemed so sure.

If Dr. Teague murdered Stuart McKay, he might have planted the knife himself to make it look like a setup to divert our attention elsewhere. A complex plan but the doctor was highly intelligent and capable of complexity.

Or, as my initial instinct suggested, someone else murdered Stuart and was framing the doctor. If that was true, the killer wasn't very adept at hiding his intention. Or else that person was blinded by anxiety and fear of exposure and making mistakes. That individual had been sitting at the Scott Supper that night. I was sure of it. If not the doctor, then one of the others.

I parked in front of the doctor's surgery and noted the closed sign in the window before letting myself through the gate leading to the garden and the shed beyond. Everything was as we'd left it yesterday. And in the light of day, I wasn't nearly so sure of Teague innocence. He was the only one who had a motive. So far.

When I returned to the sidewalk and opened the car door, Poppy, Teague's neighbor, was hustling my way, robe flapping to reveal a yellow flowery nightgown. I closed the door, stepped back on the curb, and waited.

Poppy ground to a halt and barraged me with questions, "Constable, what happened to the doctor? Did you arrest him? I saw him leave with you yesterday. Is he our murderer? What happens next? Can I help?"

"Dr. Teague is cooperating with the investigation," I repeated again. "No charges have been filed." The closed sign in the window seemed so final to me. I glanced at Poppy. Did she ever get dressed? "You're an observant woman," I said. "Have you noticed anything unusual lately in regards to the doctor or his surgery?"

"Unusual?" Her face furrowed as she considered. "Ye mean was the doc acting strange?"

"That. Or anything else that you might think was off kilter."

"There was an incident last week," She said hesitantly then waved her hand, dismissing it. "Tis nothing though."

"Anything, no matter how small, may be significant."

"Here is tis, then. It was dusk when I noticed someone peeking in the window, this one right before us with the closed sign." Poppy pointed. "I could tell the doc wasn't inside. No lights on and none above where he lives either. It might o' been a patient hoping he was available tae take a peek at an injury. Or someone wanting tae chat him up."

"You say a week ago?"

"About that."

That was before Stuart's death, so Poppy hadn't inadvertently witnessed the planting of the knife. If in fact, it had been planted. So many ifs.

"What did this person look like?"

"Couldn't tell from the distance and it was getting dark. He was wearing a dark hoodie, but I did see a bit o' blond hair sticking out, long like ruffians wear it. Now that I put my mind tae the memory, that person must o' been one o' them young trouble-makers, maybe a druggie hoping tae steal his next fix from the doctor's cupboard. I ran tae get my binoculars, but when I came back, he had disappeared."

Poppy looked worried. "Should I have called the coppers?"

"I don't see what good it would have done. As you said, he'd disappeared. Are you certain that this person was male?"

Poppy frowned in thought. "Not positive, no. But women don't wear hoodies. No-good trouble-makers do. Gang members." She paused and her eyes narrowed. "What's all this got tae do with ye taking the doctor away? Do ye have a case against him?"

"Keep an eye out," I said, as if that wasn't a given for this nosy neighbor. "And call the station if you see anything or remember anything else."

*

While I considered whether or not to make a visit to Taste of Scotland to purchase a scone, weighing the pros and cons of all those extra calories, Morag Lisle drove up next to my car and rolled down her window. Rhona was in the passenger seat.

"We had such good luck tracking the robber," Rhona called out, animated, "that we decided tae help catch the Glenkillen murderer."

"Is that right," I said, addressing the driver, realizing I sounded like the inspector when he confronted a troublesome do-gooder.

Morag squirmed, but only a little. "It was Rhona's idea. We thought we'd take a crack at it."

"You'd be interfering with an ongoing investigation," I informed them, noting that Rhona deflated a bit at that.

Morag studied me. "Rumor around the village is that Dr. Teague has been arrested for the murder."

"That's all it is. A rumor."

"That's what I thought."

"I hope he didn't do it," I blurted, shocked at such a public display of my personal opinion when I should have been professional and neutral. Then I remembered that Morag had been at the pub gathering when I'd defended him and already knew how I felt. Jamieson kept his opinions to himself, just dealing with facts as they presented themselves, and he also didn't allow himself to get close to people. But for me, the doctor had a human face; one I'd thought had been good for the village.

"Hope won't find yer killer," Morag said, with a brittle tone.

Rhona peeked up at me from her seat. "At least that clot-heid robber is off the street."

They drove off, the red-head and blue-haired duo. I left my car where it was and walked to the bookstore instead of the bakery. Dallas was unpacking a new shipment of books and arranging them in the window display. I glanced at a few titles – court room dramas, forensic thrillers, police procedurals, cozy mysteries.

"Do you actually read all of these?" I asked.

Dallas turning from her task and grinned. "As many as I can. I'm a big mystery buff, in every single sub-genre."

With all that crime fiction background, Dallas hardly would have messed up planting evidence.

"I'd like your take on Stuart," I asked her, recalling how she'd defended him after his bad behavior. "Your honest opinion."

Dallas shrugged and went back to sorting and arranging. "He came to do readings. He drew in customers. I'm a businesswoman and that means dealing with all sorts of people."

"Implying…"

"The doctor wouldn't hurt a soul," Dallas said. "Ye best look elsewhere."

And that was exactly why I was standing in the bookshop, questioning the bookseller.

Chapter 14

I had nothing constructive to show so far. I burrowed into a back warren at the Kilt & Thistle with a cup of black tea, booted up my laptop, and checked the time. How quickly twenty-four hours can pass when you're watching the minutes. My cell phone rang.

"Brenda Findlay was a nurse," the inspector said, no less abruptly than usual. "This was before she quit tae assist her husband with his accounting practice."

"A surgical nurse?" I asked, tapping down the excitement I felt building inside.

"General medical. I went over and brought that up. She claims we never asked; that it wasn't a secret, and simply an oversight on her part. O' course, Derrick backed her up."

"And she has an alibi," I pointed out, wondering how the inspector would go about cracking open an alibi like that, with husband and wife collaborating on each other's whereabouts.

"Aye." Jamieson snorted. "The clock on holding the doctor ran down, if yer wondering."

"I'd noticed. Have you charged Dr. Teague?"

"I applied fer an additional thirty-six hour hold due tae the seriousness o' the crime and was granted approval."

So, we'd bought some time.

"I'm about to do a little online searching at the pub," I told him. "See what turns up regarding the supper guests."

"Keep me apprised." And he rang off without a proper goodbye.

Minutes turned into hours as I entered names, beginning with the easiest to trace and the least likely suspects.

Dallas Irving's second-generation bookshop had excellent reviews, earning her a four-and-a-half out of five stars, and equally high praise from readers who had enjoyed her shop and shelves. One of those great reviews was my own, as the bookstore was a favorite of mine. Everything about her online referenced the shop, which I guessed was her great passion. That, and her cats.

Nothing came up for Morag Lisle, but that didn't strike me as unusual, especially if she'd lived a quiet and unassuming life. No award-winning achievements to make her stand out from the pack. No scandals to grace the social media pages. In fact, I didn't find any signs of social media activity on her part.

After a brief search, I learned that Brenda Findlay, maiden name Sutherland, had attended the University of Stirling based in the Western Isles Hospital in Stornoway, which, I read, was the largest town in the Hebrides. There, twenty-odd years ago, Brenda received her adult nursing degree and remained on at the hospital for several years post-graduation, before marrying Derrick Findlay, who worked in accounting at the hospital.

They appeared to be a perfectly regular couple, moving to Glenkillen while still newlyweds and establishing a private accounting practice. Below that slick exterior was anybody's guess. But I couldn't help making an observation in the couple's favor. It would have been unlikely that they had been acquainted with Stuart prior to meeting in Glenkillen through the Sir Walter Scott Club. There was a vast distance between the Hebrides and Edinburgh.

Brenda was certainly addicted to social media, as the inspector had learned earlier. She posted several times daily, mostly trivial activities. I scrolled through prior days but saw no status updates involving Stuart's demise, although I did find her reference to the Scott Supper and comments from others, none of whom I recognized.

Next, I turned my attention to Dr. Teague, and realized how little I knew about the man, including his first name, which I discovered was Glenn. Dr. Glenn Teague came up quickly in local news sources when he'd bought out Dr. Keen two years ago.

According to reports, he'd given up a successful career in Glasgow in exchange for a quieter setting and a chance to really get to know his patients.

"I'm pleased to be away from the hustle and bustle and rat race of Glasgow and able to concentrate on what I love best – attending to patients on a personal as well as professional level," he'd stated in one of the articles.

But when I tried to delve deeper, trace his roots back to Glasgow, I hit a solid wall. Nothing came up.

I called the inspector and explained the problem. "Can we find out whether Dr. Teague practiced under a name other than Glenn? I found an Irvine Teague at Glasgow Royal Infirmary, but no photograph of the doctor on his profile page."

"I'll see what I can do."

Fifteen minutes later, Jamieson had an answer. "The doc's middle name is Irvine." The inspector pronounced the name as Er-vin, where I'd said Er-vine. But in both cases, whatever the proper pronunciation, I'd found another link in our doctor's past employment history. And briefly wondered why he'd used his middle name then and his first name now at his surgery in Glenkillen.

I didn't have to ponder for long, because I found the answer. As Sean might say, Dr. Teague had been in a pickle and a stew. The *Glasgow Daily Times* reported that he had bungled a keyhole surgery to remove a gallbladder, wrongly cutting the patient's main bile duct and right hepatic artery. The patient, Callum Woodward, age 34, developed sepsis, failed to recover, and shortly thereafter died of complications.

Two weeks later, an updated report followed.

An investigation was conducted by Crown Prosecution Services. Criminal charges were considered, but dropped, after determining insufficient evidence to prosecute. During this same period of time, Dr. Teague resigned from the hospital staff, with speculation that he'd been forced to leave.

A few more searches and I read that his wife divorced him within the year.

I closed the laptop, stunned by this new revelation, this tiny peek into the dark corner of Teague's career. The doctor, only in his forties, should have been enjoying the prime of his life and career. Instead, he was washed out in the big city by a careless mistake. A fatal one for Callum Woodward.

I phoned the inspector.

"How am I tae get anything done when yer demanding that I play assistant tae ye?" he asked lightly. "What can I do fer ye now?"

"Just listen to what I found." And I filled him in and finished with, "Poppy Smith said Stuart barged into the surgery and called him a quack. Now we know why."

"Aye, McKay might o' found out about the botched surgery and used it against the doctor."

I sighed heavily. All I'd wanted to do was clear the doctor. Instead, I'd further incriminated him. "His reputation would be ruined if that got around Glenkillen. "Do you think Dr. Teague killed him to silence him?"

"I have enough tae charge him. We're still lacking direct evidence, and we'll have tae resort tae circumstantial tae prove intent, but that's the way it usually goes in murder cases such as this. We don't need the extra time I requested."

I wasn't quite ready to give up on the doctor. "You have him in custody. He isn't going anywhere. Let me do more digging. See what turns up. Has he requested a lawyer?"

"He's meek as a lamb. Isn't confessing. Isn't denying. It's almost as though he's accepted whatever happens next without any fight at all."

"Give me that extra time." As long as I was digging Dr. Teague's grave I might as well continue. "You wouldn't want to charge an innocent man. Even if a jury ended up acquitting him, the fact that he was charged in the first place would ruin his career here. He's already lost one practice and his marriage."

After a pause, the inspector spoke, "Another day won't hurt. And let's keep his past tae ourselves fer now. No one needs tae know about his troubles, including yer friend Vicki and her fiancée."

"I hope no one ever finds out. A man should be able to start over. Unless he goes to trial. Then everyone would know."

We'd barely disconnected when Sean entered the pub and spotted me. "Writing during a murder investigation, are ye?"

I'd never train the man to respect my privacy in my public writing spot. "How did it go?" I asked, closing the laptop.

Sean didn't take a seat this time, and I didn't offer one.

"Dallas Irving and Morag Lisle are innocent bystanders, if ye ask me. They cooperated, didn't behave suspiciously, and fer the record, I can't imagine a woman stabbing a man tae death." Sean frowned. "It's almost as though the boss is making me chase me tail while he deals with the real killer.

The doc did it. No point in sending me on wild goat chases."

"First of all, that's sexist. Women are perfectly capable of real bloodshed. I've wanted to stab certain unnamed individuals a few times myself." Wasn't that the truth? "Second, maybe Morag or Dallas saw or heard something that might be valuable to the case. The real work begins once we have a suspect in custody. Like now."

"Ye don't have tae scold me over facts I already know," Sean said. "I'm on my way tae make Andy Morris give a full confession with all the details including where he tossed the handbags."

"That sounds like a great idea. I'm going with you."

"Ye can if ye keep yer bossy ways out of it. I'm the lead on this one."

"Okay, sure."

Chapter 15

"Ye need tae tell us a bit more about the robberies," Sean said to Andy from the head of the table in the interrogation room.

"What's in it fer me?" Andy said, effecting an exaggerated slouch and a tough guy attitude.

"We can't guarantee anything," I told him. "But I'll put in a good word for you, explain how you cooperated."

Andy scoffed.

"Or," Sean added, "we can tap ye fer the murder of Stuart McKay."

Andy shot up straight, "Ye can't d...do that! And I'm taking b...back my confession. It was made under duress. Y..Ye saw what they did tae me."

"You did the right thing by telling the truth," I said, trying to soothe him before he clammed up and refused to speak at all. "And we have your knife and the mask you wore during the robberies to prove you did it."

Sean shot me a stern look, reminding me that he was supposed to be in charge. Bungling it, if you ask me. I hurried on before he could interrupt. "What did you do with the women's purses?"

"Threw them in a rubbish b...bin behind the pub. The r...rubbish has been picked up. They're gone." Andy smirked, pleased with himself.

"All right." I'd expected that. "So, let's talk about the most current robberies and how you changed your method of operation by confining them in the trunk twice in the same day."

Andy simply stared at me.

Sean cut in, "The very same day that Stuart McKay was murdered, I might add."

Andy opened his mouth, but it wasn't to clarify any details of his robberies. "I want my lawyer!" he demanded.

After that, he refused to talk.

"Progress," Sean said on the way out.

"Progress? He's lawyering up. If you hadn't badgered him about the murder, we would have all the information we need."

"He isn't getting real legal representation," Sean said. "His uncle, Bill, has been advising him."

I was astonished at the absurdity. "Bill Morris. *Our* Bill Morris?"

"Aye, the drunk. He fancies himself a bit of a legal mind."

"And exactly what is Bill advising?"

"Bill told him to own up tae it and get his arse back tae work at the inn."

"But confessing isn't going to get him back to work," I said. "And that's hardly what an attorney would advise."

Outside, the sky had suddenly turned black and the wind howled, bending trees and lashing the plantings outside Glenkillen's businesses.

"Best get inside someplace tae weather this out," Sean called, holding onto his cap as we exited the station.

I ran to my car and sat inside for a few moments, watching Mother Nature's incredible power as Sean pulled away. Violent storms came up quickly in the village, first forming over the sea then spiraling inland. Lights up and down the street flickered and went out. There was no reason to

157

return to my online search at the pub unless power was restored momentarily.

Lights remained out as I waited.

Then I remembered Leith. He was out to sea, and this time, he'd had no warning of a brewing storm. I drove to the harbor, windshield wipers beating as fast as they would go, peering through the sheets of rain as best I could.

The North Sea was an angry, swirling, black beast with enormous waves crashing into the lighthouse that guarded the harbor entrance. Our inlet, Moray Firth, raged as well.

Fear gripped me. How could a boat the size of *Bragging Rights* survive this driving wind and rain? Leith was a seasoned sailor and had emergency gear on board, but would that be enough? On an afternoon excursion, Leith had given me the tour - life vests, flares for distress signals, anchors, oars and paddles in case of engine failure, radios.

Radios! Perhaps he'd used a marine frequency to make a distress call. But in this weather, no one in their right mind would attempt a rescue. What about all the other fishermen out there?

Feeling helpless, I drove cautiously back to the farm. Torrential rains continued with driving winds.

I ran for Vicki's door and was drenched before I made it inside. Power was out there, too, and Vicki had lit candles. She handed me a towel. Sean poured tea for me.

"Leith is out there!" I said in dismay, sinking into a kitchen chair.

"He's seen the likes o' this before," Sean reassured me, then to Vicki, "Remember the Eyemouth Disaster?"

Vicki gave him a warning glance, her hands wrapped around her teacup for warmth. "Not a story for right now."

But Sean was already relating it. "1881. The worst fishing disaster. 189 lives lost at sea, either capsized or crashed into the rocks at the harbor entrance."

"Sean!" Vicki said, her voice warning him.

"They referred tae it as Black Friday." One glance at Vicki's expression and Sean said, "All right. I'll stop."

Vicki leaned forward and covered my hand with hers. "No sense working yourself up about a thing you can't control. Leith's isn't the only boat out there. The fishermen will look out for each other. He'd be wise to ride out the storm rather than

159

rushing toward home against the forces. Trying to escape the storm would be the worst thing he could do."

A little later, I went to my own cottage to hole up with Snookie. I made a fire to ward off the chill and it created enough light to read by. But I couldn't concentrate.

Late afternoon turned into evening and the storm continued to rage, leaving me wondering how long the power would be out. I couldn't stop thinking about Leith and what he was enduring. Whether he was still alive or if he'd gone to an underwater grave. If his boat had capsized, what would have happened to Kelly, who always accompanied him on his excursions? And what about the fishermen he'd taken out?

I was almost physically ill from apprehension.

This was exactly the scenario he'd described when giving me reasons why he didn't want to have a woman waiting for him at home. What he hadn't considered was the effect his disappearance would have on the rest of us – his friends and his family. What about his daughter, Fia?

Sometime through the night I fell asleep in the chair. When I awoke, the fire had gone out, the storm had passed, power had been restored, and dawn had broken.

Chapter 16

After a cup of coffee, I attempted to call Leith, but got no answer. Slipping on a thick fleece and a pair of old Wellingtons donated to me by Vicki, I set out for the moor for a brisk walk to clear my head before facing whatever the day would bring.

I was worried about Leith, but debated what to do next, if there was anything at all to do. Carry on, I guess. Work on the case. Stay busy until word came.

Sheep are naturally inquisitive and an entire flock turned and watched me as I marched down the lane and turned up into the heathered hills.

I struggled to force my attention to the murder case. Sharing one of my theories and casting suspicion amongst the club members hadn't produced a single shred of new evidence. None of them had come forward to point an accusatory finger at another.

Derrick may or may not have told Stuart he was no longer welcome in the club, perhaps inciting anger in the professor, thus possibly coming to blows and death. Brenda's background as a nurse would have given her the skill to place the knife in exactly the right position for an immediate kill. Whether she had or not was unknown.

Dallas had no motive. Nor did Morag, who was the only one with a solid alibi.

Everything pointed to Dr. Teague.

So why was I resisting filing criminal charges?

The flame that had kept me in pursuit of the truth had dimmed with the storm and my friend's unknown fate at its hand. The day seemed bleak, even as the sun broke over the ridge, illuminating the lush vegetation surrounding me.

Leith's friendly coo didn't make an appearance either, shrouding the hills in even more gloom.

Back at the cottage, I fed Snookie, ate a stale scone and washed it down with several more cups of coffee. After a quick shower, I headed out. The Peugeot steered in the direction of the harbor as though I were merely a passenger.

Locals had congregated at the dock. Joining them on the weathered wooden planks, with the sun above and the sound of riggings filling the air, it might have been a regular day by the sea. Sparkling sun danced on the waters of the firth. Many fishing boats were docked, but several slips were vacant, including Leith's.

Two weathered sailors huddled together at the end of one of the piers and I made my way over to them to request news.

"Search party went out at first light," one of them told me. "Three boats didn't come in. The rest made it back following the storm. We're monitoring radio channels for distress signals. Two of them reported in."

"Was one Leith Cameron?" I asked, anxiously.

Two heads shook in unison, giving me my answer. Leith was the only one not heard from.

As much as I wanted to stay at the harbor and wait it out, this was the last day to investigate before Dr. Teague was formally charged, and I wanted to make a good showing. If only I knew where to start.

It was too early to seek out club members and Glenkillen businesses weren't open yet, so I drove to the police station and found Jamieson at his desk reviewing files.

"I heard about Leith Cameron," he said, his sharp eyes studying my face.

"I just came from the harbor. A search is underway. He's the only one who hasn't radioed in."

"Do ye want tae take some time off?" he asked, his Scottish accent soft and understanding.

"I'm worried, I admit it. But sitting around doing nothing would be intolerable. I'd like to speak with the doctor. And since I'm here, I want a word with Andy."

"Ye want me tae sit in? Although I haven't accomplished much with either o' them."

I spotted Sean entering the building. "No, I can handle this and definitely don't suggest that Sean go in with me."

The inspector raised an eyebrow. "And here I thought ye were the lad's biggest supporter."

"Have ye charged the doctor?" Sean asked, ambling into the room. "And how about our car robber?"

"Andy Morris has been charged," the inspector said. "And as tae the doctor, we'll finish out the day with more investigating before we take that action."

Sean wore a slightly disappointed expression. "There's nothin' more tae do. He's the one."

"Constable Elliott has a few ideas," Jamieson said.

I did? That was news to me.

"I'll help her then," Sean said. The inspector and I exchanged glances. I hope I conveyed the plea I couldn't voice.

Jamieson came through. "I need ye down at the harbor. Leith Cameron is still unaccounted for and ye are tae keep us informed as tae progress. If I need ye fer the murder case, I'll pull ye from the dock."

Sean's eyebrows knitted in confusion. "Ye want me at the harbor?"

"Aye, and make it quick."

"Wear sunscreen," I advised Sean, glad that someone would be on hand at that scene. The Scottish fair skin couldn't handle the sun's harsh rays and I didn't want Sean abandoning his post because of a bad burn.

Sean left, grumbling under his breath.

I smiled. "You had breakfast this morning, didn't you?"

"Ye want a growl, I can give ye one."

"I'll take that as a yes. You're a changed man when your blood sugar is in check."

"I'll get our jailbird." Jamieson rose.

Several minutes later, he brought the doctor into the interrogation room where I waited, handcuffed him to a chair, and departed. I presumed that he would be watching and listening to our conversation from the other side of the mirror.

Dr. Teague's shoulders slumped and his demeanor implied that he had given up, accepting whatever fate awaited him. His face was haggard, and his eyes didn't meet mine.

"Doctor," I began, "we don't have much time, so I will get right to the point. We are aware of the circumstances surrounding your resignation in Glasgow. I would like to know how Stuart McKay learned of it."

The doctor stared at his feet. "It isn't a hard thing tae learn if ye search a wee bit. Ye found out yerself in no time at all. It's that most people, patients I'm referring tae, don't bother with searching a person's past unless they want tae use it

167

fer no good. That was a hobby tae McKay, especially if he wanted tae cause pain."

"That's why he came to the surgery and called you names?"

"Quack? Aye. He was holding it over my head, threatening tae tell my patients."

"So that begs the question. Did you murder Stuart to silence him?"

The doctor looked up at the mirror behind which Jamieson was sure to be standing. "No! I did not kill Stuart McKay."

"Your neighbor, Poppy, related an incident that occurred last week. Someone dressed in a hoodie was peering in the window at the surgery. It was at dusk so Poppy didn't get a good look, but she thought the individual was acting suspicious."

Teague shrugged indifferently and studied his feet again. "It might have been anyone. A patient hoping to catch me in, perhaps fer a consultation."

I went on, "Doctor, if you are as innocent as you claim, then someone planted the murder weapon on your property hoping we would find it. A suspicious character was seen in the vicinity before the murder, possibly surveying the surgery and garden. That would suggest premeditation. Not only was Stuart McKay a victim, but if what you say is true, you yourself are about to become the next victim. You might not be losing your life, but you will lose your freedom. Don't you care enough to fight?"

This time the doctor glanced at me. "I was beside myself with grief when I learned what I had done tae my patient. And what I'd done tae his family. It was inexcusable. I resigned from the hospital and seriously considered never practicing medicine again. But all I know is how to help people, so I quietly moved tae Glenkillen when I learned of the surgery being available and bought it. Here, I administer at a much lower level where I can't hurt anybody like I did before.

"My days of operating are at an end. I try tae make amends in small ways, stitching up minor cuts and setting broken bones. But in the end, maybe I deserve what's happening tae me fer being so arrogant as tae think I could continue treating patients in any manner."

I didn't know what to say. The doctor was in such pain. He was responsible for at least one death, and he was suffering terribly. His speech to me was heartfelt, and I wanted to believe him, but still the evidence against him was powerfully strong.

More and more, I was convinced that the doctor was being framed. But another, more sinister idea came into focus.

It was possible that Stuart McKay's murder was a means to a different end. Maybe he wasn't really the intended target. Stuart was an unlikeable character, so we'd assumed someone he'd provoked had killed him. But maybe the doctor wasn't just a convenient way to shift blame from the real killer. Could this have been carefully planned out from the very beginning to bring down the doctor?

"Give me something to go on," I said, quietly. "Who would do this to you?"

Dr. Teague stared at me. "I have no idea. Are ye really saying ye believe that I'm innocent?"

"I think that's a reasonable possibility. And the killer could very well be someone from your own past."

Chapter 17

I was in such a hurry to further investigate the doctor's history that I raced out of the building, disregarding the inspector and forgetting about my earlier request to speak with Andy Morris. At the Kilt & Thistle, I set up my laptop behind a thick stone column in a back warren where no one would look for me. Then I began another online search.

I went back and reread news reports of the death of Callum Woodward, Teague's patient who had died from sepsis. Both of the deceased man's parents, Lorna and Ivar Woodward, had been interviewed after the pursuit of charges against the doctor had been dropped.

"Callum would have agreed with the final outcome," Ivar stated. "We wish the doctor no ill will."

Lorna concurred. "It was a tragic accident, one we must all learn to live with."

I searched specifically for images, hoping to find photographs of them, and was rewarded with several. Neither would have stood out in a crowd. But I was certain I'd never seen either of them in Glenkillen.

I called the inspector.

"Well, if it isn't the sprinter who blew out o' the station earlier."

"I had something to do. Can we look into the family of Dr. Teague's patient, the one who died after surgery? Parents' names are Ivar and Lorna Woodward. Patient was Callum Woodward. I might be grasping at straws, but I'd like to know where they were when Stuart McKay was killed."

The inspector sighed heavily. "Ye suspect the parents o' the murder?"

"You listened to my interview with Dr. Teague, right?"

"Aye."

"Then you understand why I'm looking into the doctor's past. The parents were pretty forgiving in the newspaper articles I just read. I doubt that they had anything to do with it. But what about a girlfriend? Or other family members who might have been seeking revenge? Maybe Brenda and Derrick

Findlay are related to the Woodward's somehow. We're looking for someone who wasn't as quick as the parents to forgive."

"I'll see what I can do through law enforcement in Glasgow."

"Thank you, and, uh, any word down at the dock?"

"Ye'll be the first tae know."

I phoned Vicki shortly after to update her on Leith's situation and to let her know that Sean was at the harbor.

"I'll take Sean some lunch," she said. "A nice warm smoked haddock bake will do him good. There's more here if you want to stop home and eat."

"No thanks. I'm on a roll and don't want to waste a minute."

I gathered up my personal belongings and headed for the front of the pub, where Bill sat at his usual table. The two of us had been civil with each other up to this point, but today Bill shot me the evil eye.

"And good day to you, too," I said, when he continued to glare.

Bill shook his head as though finding something hard to believe. "I thought ye were the good one," he said. "But yer just as bad as him."

As bad as the inspector, I assumed. "We didn't have a choice in arresting your nephew. Andy robbed those women. He's confessed. I thought that's what you yourself advocated."

"Aye, but ye are trying tae make him admit tae things he didn't do."

"He isn't accused of murdering Stuart McKay."

"It's been brought up by that wee copper with the big boasts."

"Officer Stevens has reversed his position." Which wasn't true. Sean believed in the doctor's guilt wholeheartedly.

"But murder isn't all I'm referring tae, not that I'm talking tae you at all. Trumping up, ye are. Yer just as bad."

For some reason that stung. I'd gone out of my way to befriend all the locals. And I'd never bullied anyone to get them to confess to anything. I tried to be the epitome of decorum when working as a special constable and always deferred to the inspector when the situation called for a bad guy. A role he didn't seem to mind.

"What are you talking about?" I asked, coaxing.

But Bill was done. His lips were set in a hard line.

As I left the pub, I almost ran into Rhona.

"The hobby bobby," she exclaimed. "Just the person I'm looking for."

"Now what?" was on the tip of my tongue as I was feeling tense and rushed and disliked. Time was running out. Leith was missing. And whatever small amount of cordiality that had existed between Bill and myself had evaporated.

Wait. What had she just called me?

"Hobby bobby?" I said coldly, as she turned and followed me.

"I meant it in an affectionate way," Rhona explained. "In fact, I want tae apply for a position. I figure if ye can do it, so can I. Catching that robber opened my eyes to my true calling."

"You're retired. You don't need a calling." I stopped and shifted the tote containing my laptop to the other shoulder. "I'm really in a hurry. Can we talk about this another time?" Like never.

But the pensioner wouldn't give up, a personality trait that had gotten her locked in the trunk of her own car. "I have information about that murder that you could use."

A new voice piped up, rather loudly. "Information about the murder?"

Morag Lisle appeared on the street and had overheard us.

"Shhh." Rhona frowned. "Not so loud. And yer late."

"I couldn't find my car keys. Searched all over before they showed up."

Rhona addressed me, "It's nothing at all that I know. Forget I said anything."

I hurried past the amateur sleuth team. Apparently, warning them away from the murder investigation was futile. Besides, if those two actually discovered something worthwhile to contribute, how could that hurt?

"What information?" I heard Morag asked. The answer blew away with the closing of the door. I seriously doubted that Rhona would tell Morag about her request to become a special constable. She would worry about the potential for competition for the non-existent position.

I imagined Rhona on the force. The inspector would go stark raving mad.

Chapter 18

The inspector was in his office, long legs on top of his desk, ankles crossed, talking on the phone. I sidled in without an invitation and sat down across from him.

The conversation was one-sided, Jamieson listening. Or perhaps he'd been put on hold. There was nothing for me to do but wait.

"Thank ye fer yer assistance," he said, finally hanging up. He removed his feet from the desk, glanced at a clock on the wall, and addressed me, "Didn't I chust speak tae ye moments ago?"

"I was at the pub. It's a hop and a skip away. What have you got?"

"Since I spoke tae ye? Nothing o' significance yet. Glasgow is willing tae gather the requested information regarding the Woodard family, but it'll take time."

"We don't have time!"

Jamieson held up his hands. "Slow down. Yer working yerself into a snit. We have this day and many days after this one tae make or break a case."

"You are rushing an arrest! I understand the pressure you must be under to solve this but…"

An eyebrow shot up. "We have damning evidence. The bloody smoking gun. Ye'd let him loose, would ye?"

"This will ruin his career."

"He did that tae himself."

We glared at each other. Then his appearance softened. "I know yer feeling let down. Disappointed in the human race, refusing tae believe the doctor is capable o' murder. But facts are facts, and ye can't stuff them in a box when it suits ye."

"You don't believe he's innocent." The expression on his face told me I'd guessed correctly. "You've been humoring me? Giving me the day to run around trying to prove he's innocent when all along you plan to charge him?"

"Ye need more time tae accept it, and I'm giving ye what I can. Glasgow will get back tae us on the whereabouts o' the patient's parents and a rundown on friends and family. Ye'll see that they weren't in Glenkillen, killing Stuart McKay. And ye'll be left with Teague."

"Unbelievable!"

I rose and stomped out, jumped in the Peugeot, and wiped away a tear. The inspector and I had never argued before. In the past, our views had usually coincided, not collided. We'd been able to read each other's thoughts and intentions. Not this time. I was a rookie and he'd let me run out to the end of my rope. I'd been tethered all along and hadn't been aware of it. I was angry and felt betrayed.

I drove to the harbor where many of the fishing and sailing boats had left the dock for the day, leaving most of the slips empty. Vicki and Sean greeted me from the end of the dock where the two sailors I'd met earlier were still watching the sea for news.

"Any word?" I asked, addressing anyone who might want to respond.

"Nothing," Sean said. "This would be my most boring assignment tae date, if Vicki hadn't appeared tae keep me company."

Vicki rummaged in a basket at her feet and brought out a covered dish. "I brought an extra plate of smoked haddock bake and it's still warm. Sit."

I plopped on a bench and accepted the meal, took a bite, and told her it was good, which was the best I could offer considering my emotional state and my inability to taste anything.

"Haddock," Sean said. "Potatoes, spring onions, broad beans, a few secret spices known only tae Vicki, and a cheesy crust on top. Eat it up and it'll change yer mood from sour tae sweet. Ye must be keen on a good meal."

"You need to stay optimistic," Vicki said a minute or two later.

I swallowed and composed myself. "Everything is going wrong. Dr. Teague will be charged with murder, and I'd hoped he was innocent, Andy is a criminal, and Bill has decided I'm some kind of crooked cop, Leith and Kelly are missing along with the fishermen he took out, and I fear the outcome…"

"Now, now," Sean interrupted. "Yer letting yer mind take over and think the worst. Here's the truth. The doctor deserves tae be charged, we're glad tae have the robber behind bars, and Cameron will make it in."

I continued to sulk while they walked down the pier, hand-in-hand, heads together in hushed conversation. I stood, placed the empty plate in the basket, and gazed out toward the lighthouse where several boats, motorized and sailboat alike, were vying for space to go out and come into the inlet.

"Me eyes are playing tricks," one of the men down the pier shouted. "I do believe that's Cameron's fishing boat coming this way."

The other used binoculars to scan the water. I ran over.

"Aye, that's his."

I interrupted, "Can you see him? And the fishermen? And Kelly?"

After another moment, he said, "All accounted fer. And that's the search boat trailing behind them."

I actually jumped for joy. Then ran over to Leith's slip and waited impatiently for the boat to arrive. Vicki and Sean stood beside me as Leith pulled in and threw a line to Sean, who cleated it securely. The search boat went on further down the pier and tucked into another slip.

Leith grinned up at me, and I would have thrown smoked haddock bake at him if I hadn't eaten it all. Or been so happy. How dare he grin when we've been worried sick!

Kelly leapt from the boat. After helping his clients onto the dock and sending them away, Leith turned to us. The grin dropped.

"Those blokes almost got us killed out there," he said. "One o' them dropped the radio overboard in the worst moments o' the storm. The other smashed the GPS unit, don't ask me how. And I practically had to strap them down on opposite sides of the boat to keep us from capsizing, both o' them running tae the same side at once."

"They're large boys," Vicki observed.

"Aye, and so, due tae their incompetence, I didn't know which direction was home and had no way to call for help. If it wasn't fer the search crew, we would have been lost at sea indefinitely."

I gave Leith a huge hug.

"Worried, were ye?" he whispered playfully in my ear, hugging me back.

"Not a bit," I said, lying as I released him. "I was told you are a superior sailor and would outlast the storm." That part was true.

"I told her ye'd make it," Sean said, slightly braggy, standing next to *Bragging Rights*.

"I've been out in worse." Leith said while wrapping more lines snuggly. "But then I had assistance, not those bumbling mates." He finished securing lines. "I need to go see Fia then get some sleep. And I'm cancelling fishing trips for the next few days. I'll be in touch soon."

With the Border collie in the lead, the four of us walked off the pier together, Sean a few steps behind, speaking on his phone. Vicki and Leith got into their respective vehicles and pulled away from the harbor. Sean met me at my car. "I gave the good news tae the inspector. He says ye should take the day tae do whatever ye like. He knows how much Cameron means tae ye."

"He's a friend," I muttered, wondering what Jamieson believed was going on between the two of us.

But Sean didn't hear and went on, "Me? I'm tae report in." He frowned in thought. "Not that there'll be much tae do, what with both cases solved."

I gazed toward the dock, at the peaceful waves lapping at the shoreline, knowing one of the cases wasn't quite finished. At least in my book.

"Tell the inspector I still expect to have my day."

"What do ye mean?"

"Just tell him."

I climbed into my car and leaned back against the headrest. Both cases were solved, according to two law officials who knew more than I did about solving crimes. The inspector was thorough and he'd passed judgement. Who was I to disagree?

Yet, I couldn't help thinking that nothing was completely resolved. Except Leith's return. I was grateful for that, more than I could say.

I intended to follow through with my plan to continue investigating.

Regardless of today's outcome, though, tomorrow would find me back at my favorite table at the Kilt & Thistle writing love scenes. It was time to return to my work. I'd had enough of murder and mayhem. I could do with a little love.

Chapter 19

Brenda opened the door when I rang the bell. She wasn't as hospitable toward me as she'd been. The door didn't swing wide, welcoming me in. This time, I wasn't invited inside the Crannog Lane home where she'd hosted the fatal supper.

"What do ye want now?" she asked from behind a partially closed door.

"I was hoping to have a word with you." I'd intended to ask her about her nursing career, but feared she'd slam the door in my face.

"Do ye still believe that one of us killed Stuart and left the doctor tae take the rap? He's been nicked fer the crime, a crime he must have committed."

"He's incarcerated at the moment, yes." I tried to peek past her. "Is Derrick inside?"

"No, and that's the reason I'm not allowing ye in. We stand together."

186

I nodded in understanding, well aware. "When will he return?"

"I'm not sure." Brenda began to close the door, then must have reconsidered because she pushed it open a bit more. "Do you know your Sir Walter Scott?"

"Only a little." I dredged up a quote. "*Is death the last step? No, it is the final awakening.*"

I'd managed to elicit an expression of satisfaction. "Apropos," she said, obviously obsessed with the Scottish writer. "*To the timid and hesitating everything is impossible because it seems so.*"

"He was a deep thinker," I agreed.

Then her face changed quickly from pleasure to disapproval. "Ye know, Morag Lisle claims she went tae university fer English studies and especially fer Sir Walter Scott, yet she didn't recognize a famous passage Derrick quoted. The schools aren't doing a proper job of educating; not like they used tae."

"Yes, well, I'll come back later," I said. "But could you at least tell me if you know two names I'd like to pass by you?"

"Doesn't seem any harm in that."

"Lorna and Ivar Woodward."

Brenda paused in thought. "Woodward. The names don't ring a bell. Are they from Glenkillen?"

"Glasgow."

"She shook her head and said convincingly, "Never heard of them."

As I made my way along the sloping path to the lane, I recalled the conversation that Brenda had referred to.

"Time will rust the sharpest sword," Derrick had said. Morag and I had asked for clarification.

I'd heard the quote before and had only been surprised with the reference since the topic had been Stuart's murder, and I didn't understand what a Scott quote had to do with anything. In the same manner, Morag might have been startled and questioning the relevance.

My next stop was Taste of Scotland where I purchased a dark chocolate cherry scone and a cream bun. These delicacies are better known in the United States as cream puffs. I wolfed down the scone with tea while sitting at a small café table outside of the shop. The cream bun would be a backup when hunger set in. Tomorrow, along with returning to my writing cave, I would consider healthier options.

As I finished, Sean called my cell phone. "The inspector isn't answering my calls."

That wasn't anything new. "What's up?"

"Andy's ready tae talk."

"I'll be right there."

*

"You should speak to us with your lawyer present," I advised Andy, who wasn't quite as cocky and slouchy as last time we'd met at the interrogation table. I made the suggestion because I didn't want Andy to claim coercion later.

"I don't have one really. It was a bluff." He sat up straight. "I'm willing tae be honest about what I did in exchange fer leniency."

"Ye should have representation," Sean said. "Yer facing prison time, leniency or no."

"I'm going to record this meeting," I told Andy when he insisted on continuing without an attorney. I glanced at the recording unit I'd turned on when I'd entered the room, thinking 'better late in informing him than never'.

He nodded in assent, looking worried. "Just so we're clear, I didn't kill that bloke."

I shot a warning glance at Sean, remembering how he'd bullied Andy. "We don't suspect you, Andy."

I'd already given Sean the classic zipped-lip motion to keep Andy's stories flowing without rude interruptions. He caught on, and so we listened quietly, other than a prompt to continue here and there from me.

Andy began with the first several robberies, detailing the crimes including the dates, times, locations, and descriptions of the victims and their cars. Everything fit with what we already knew. He also confirmed again that he had tossed their mobiles and purses once he'd helped himself to the contents.

Eventually, we got to Rhona Selkirk. "Then there was that blue-haired old lady. None o' the others gave me any trouble, not with a knife pointed at them. But that one! The oldest of the bunch too. She got all cheeky and threatened me. Kicked me in the shin, she did. Wouldn't stop pounding at me with those little fists until I picked her up and locked her in the boot. And tae top it off, she had nothing in her purse tae have bothered with. Same with most of them. All cards these days, even with the pensioners."

Andy Morris had just confirmed my original suspicion. He wasn't the brightest of the bright. He'd robbed at knife point for a few pounds in cash and kept doing what didn't work until he got caught.

"What about Morag Lisle?" I asked.

"Who?"

"The last one you robbed, later the same day, number two, the red-head with the grey Vauxhall Corsa."

"Shove off," Andy said violently with curled lip, his personality turning to ugly. "I said I'd be straight with ye and I expected the same in return."

Puzzled by his reaction, I said, "You've cooperated until now. Why stop?"

But Andy only glared. He stood up, kicking his chair away. "We're done."

Sean rose also, his hand on the belt above his baton in case he needed it. "I'll take ye back until ye can be civil like ye were before. Ye have an anger issue, ye do."

"Andy, sit down, please." I had a pretty good idea what was going on. My heart was racing, whether from excitement or trepidation, I didn't know. But I needed Andy to say the words. "If I have figured out something inaccurately, you need to correct me," I told him. "The recorder is running. This is your chance. Tell me what's going on."

Andy ignored the request to rejoin me at the table, but he leaned over and stared at the recorder. Then he spoke very precisely and carefully. "That crazy little lady was the last one. And I told meself so. I vowed tae retire from hitting up old ladies. I didn't do anything more that day or any day since."

"Ye did it…" Sean began.

I interrupted and rose. "Thank you for clearing that up, Andy. I'll see what I can do to help you with a lighter sentence." Then to Sean. "You can take him back to his cell now. And would you get me the address and contact information for Morag Lisle." I thought a moment. "And for Rhona Selkirk also."

"Well, aren't ye the boss lady all o' a sudden."

"And find out what you can about Morag Lisle."

"Keep ye wig on. I only have two hands."

Chapter 20

I don't remember my legs carrying me out to my car. Deep in thought, I sat in the driver's seat, staring sightlessly, my mind working overtime.

Morag Lisle had lied about the robbery. She'd used it as an alibi, claiming she'd been in the trunk of her car for hours. We hadn't questioned her statement. Not for a single moment. We'd assumed the event had occurred and moved on to other suspects. Exactly as she'd planned.

But why would she do that? Either she had invented an alibi out of fear of being wrongly accused, or she'd planned Stuart McKay's murder as well as an escape route. It was a pretty elaborate scheme.

But how could she have known about Andy stashing Rhona in the trunk, if the same hadn't happened to her? Morag and Rhona hadn't met until later when Rhona accused Andy in the bar. And the local paper hadn't printed about the latest attack, because that robbery had only occurred a few hours earlier.

Wait.

Morag had been at the bookstore with Dallas and Vicki.

That must account for her knowing.

I turned my thoughts back to that afternoon, sitting in the Kilt & Thistle. Sean had been about to pick up Vicki. The inspector arrived with news of another robbery, telling us about the victim being forced into the boot. I'd offered to drive Vicki home, and Sean said he'd let her know.

From the car, I called Vicki. When she answered, I immediately asked, "When Sean called you the afternoon of the supper to tell you I'd be picking you up at the bookshop, did he tell you he was going to another robbery?"

There was a slight hesitation on the other end before, "Hello to you, too."

"It's important, Vicki."

"Let me think." She sighed heavily. "Yes, Sean said he was on his way to the scene of another pensioner robbery."

"Did he also mention that the woman who owned the car had been locked in the boot?"

"Yes, he did. What's going on?"

"I'll explain later. This is time sensitive. And did you repeat that information to Dallas?"

There was a pause.

"It's okay if you did. I just need to know."

"I believe I did tell her, since it was even more concerning than the others. Wielding a knife is bad enough, but then to lock an old woman up like that. I can't imagine what she must have gone through."

"Who else heard you besides Dallas? Was Morag there, too?"

"Yes, she was."

"Thanks. You've helped explain something that baffled me."

After reassuring her, reiterating that she'd done nothing wrong and that I would bring her up to date when I had more time, I disconnected.

Then I put in a call to Morag's mobile number. She didn't answer and I didn't leave a message.

Next, I tried Rhona's home number as she didn't own a mobile phone. A woman with a younger voice than Rhona's answered.

"She isn't here," she said.

"And you are?"

"Her daughter. Would you like tae leave a message?"

"When do you expect her back?"

"No idea. I went out fer a spell and she was gone when I got back. Her car is here so she must be with Morag, her new best friend. My mother is a free spirit. I can't keep track of her."

I laughed politely. "That describes her perfectly."

I started the Peugeot and headed toward Laurel Crescent with the address for Morag supplied by Sean.

A sense of foreboding rode along in the passenger seat beside me.

It occurred to me on the way that I should contact the inspector and warn him of a potential situation. But I was still upset with him and told myself that Sean would fill him in as soon as he found him. Even though Sean believed that Andy had been lying, I knew he would give Jamieson the facts as he'd heard them. I'd also left the recording unit on the inspector's desk requesting that he listen to the last few minutes first. He could then form his own opinion.

In the meantime, I'd go on investigating one particular supper-goer, the last-minute Sir Walter Scott enthusiast.

I pulled up beside a single-story, red brick bungalow with dormer windows. I climbed out and rang a bell on the door while surveying the street. There wasn't any sign of Morag's car. A hunched elderly woman answered.

"I'm looking for Morag Lisle."

"And ye are?"

I showed her my credentials. "You are smart to be wary of strangers. Always make sure they are who they say they are." Then I recognized the irony of my statement. Who exactly *was* Morag Lisle? Had I asked for identification?

"May I come in?" I asked.

"Certainly."

She showed me into a small living space where I noted stairs on the left, leading up to a loft. "Would you like tea?" she asked.

"No thank you. I don't have much time." I remained on my feet although she offered a chair.

"Morag isn't here. She left early."

"How long will she be staying with you?"

"Until the investigation is over. She told me she was at the supper and is a suspect, as are the other guests. I had renters arriving yesterday, but I've had tae put them on hold. A very messy arrangement."

"Morag had planned to leave here yesterday?"

"Originally, aye, going back tae Edinburgh."

I really didn't know what to ask Morag's landlady without arousing her suspicions about Morag, and that seemed premature. While I hesitated, she said, "Would ye like tae see her room? It's above, in the loft."

I tried not to appear surprised by her offer. I managed to keep my voice neutral, "Yes, of course, that would be good."

"Yer wondering why I'd offer, and the reason is because yer here looking fer answers. If Morag has secrets, ye should know about them. We're a small community and have tae look out fer each other. Go on. I'll busy myself in the kitchen."

I climbed the steps slowly. I had the owner's permission, making a search perfectly legal. At least, I assumed so. I stepped off onto the landing and glanced around the room. Everything was tidy and put away where it belonged. I opened each dresser drawer. All were empty except the top right drawer which contained intimate apparel. The closet housed several tops on hangers and two pair of shoes on the floor neatly aligned.

This tenant could pack up and be gone in a matter of minutes.

I found a suitcase tucked under the bed, slid it out, and popped it open. Tucked at the very bottom under a stack of folded pants and more tops was a long blond wig and a hoodie.

I'd discovered the identity of Poppy's neighborhood lurker.

Slamming down the steps, items in hand, I warned the landlady to phone me as soon as Morag arrived. "Please don't tell her about my visit and place the call to me in private."

"I understand," she said, staring at the wig and hoodie. "I had a feeling something was off with that woman. Too bad it didn't strike me in the interview when she first applied. I usually can tell. She fooled me."

"She might have a perfectly sound explanation once I have a chance to interview her." Which was one big lie. Morag was anything but innocent. But was she dangerous? I wasn't sure.

Before driving off, I called the inspector rather than wait for him to listen to the recording.

He answered and I related the interview with Andy and my discovery in Morag's room.

"Anything back yet on the Woodward family members?" I asked.

"Nothing yet. I'm two hours or so from Glenkillen. Don't do anything rash before I get back."

"Of course not."

"I mean it, Eden."

I smiled. He hadn't called me Eden in a long while. I liked it better than Constable Elliott, which was so formal and removed. Necessary though, for decorum. What was his given name? Kevin, I recalled. I couldn't imagine calling him that.

Actually, I felt a tremendous sense of relief. Jamieson could take over. I'd be his assistant, which was much less nerve racking. Besides, the man's steel nerves were a source of comfort. "I'm waiting on you," I assured him.

And I meant it. I really did.

Until I remembered my last conversation with Rhona outside of the pub. She'd said she had information on the murder. And she'd made that claim within Morag's earshot. Then she'd instantly reversed and said she didn't.

Had she really had information valuable to the case?

I'd been in such a rush, I'd ignored her. Mainly because she'd just inquired about a position as a special constable, and I recall thinking she was trying to ingratiate herself with false claims.

But perhaps she'd had something on Morag. Those two had been tight lately. Something might have slipped. Morag had found out that Rhona was talking to me about the murder.

Now, suddenly, neither woman was available.

Where were they? And why were they missing?

I reeled at one gut-wrenching possibility.

Chapter 21

I didn't know where to start looking for them. Driving around wasn't going to work.

I began to drive around anyway, through the village center, past the harbor, through neighborhoods.

My cell phone alerted me to a call from Sean.

Driving and talking on a mobile is illegal in Scotland. No excuses allowed and hefty fines or revocation of driving licenses. But I didn't have a choice. These were desperate times. Besides, I *was* the police.

I answered, continuing on aimlessly.

"Yer Morag Lisle is a professional gambler," Sean said.

"Really? She never mentioned it." Although, I hadn't asked her about her background, either.

"Slick with the cards. Have ye spoken tae her?"

"I've been to the room she's renting, but she wasn't there. The landlady said she left early. Rhona isn't home, either."

I screeched to a halt, feeling helpless. "I need to find Morag as quickly as possible. Rhona could be with her. I'm sensing something bad is about to happen!"

"I might be able tae help. Lisle's vehicle has a registered address, a cottage, just shy o' the village o' Dornoch, thirty kilometers or so up the coast."

"I've been to Dornoch with Vicki."

"Then ye know tae take A9. Ye have GPS, right? I'll get ye the address. Here it is. 124 Beach Road."

"Relay this information to the inspector. I'm going to lose coverage soon. I'm down to one bar."

I plugged in the numbers and took off. Sean might not have perfected his people skills, but he was turning into a valuable asset with his research abilities.

Thirty kilometers. Roughly eighteen miles. If I drove fast, I could be there in twenty minutes.

Morag had said she lived in Edinburgh. Another lie.

Heading for the cottage was only a guess, the only lead I had, and if I was wrong, well…I couldn't focus on what might happen to Rhona. If it hadn't already occurred. A cottage tucked away from sight would be the perfect place for another murder.

But what was Morag Lisle's connection to Stuart or Teague? Why had she been snooping around the doctor's surgery? And why hadn't she been on our short list to begin with?

The first two answers eluded me, but I knew the last one. Because we'd thought that Stuart was the actual target. And because we were too quick to blame Dr. Teague. And because Morag had the only solid alibi.

Until we caught the robber.

I'd known a professional gambler in the states. He made his living based on wit. He wasn't afraid to take risks, was overly confident in his ability to control situations, and was extremely disciplined.

Morag had been checking out the surgery prior to the supper, leaving me certain that he was her intended victim. Perhaps she'd planned to kill the doctor after the supper. Then McKay and Teague had argued. Stuart wouldn't have made a good impression with Morag. In fact, he hadn't, based on her reaction at the time. She left right after the doctor had.

Had her attention really shifted from Teague to McKay in such a short period of time?

Professional gamblers were also quick on their feet. She could have revised a new plan in the blink of an eye, deciding that seeing the doctor in prison for a murder he didn't commit would be more satisfying than seeing him dead.

Ten minutes out from the address, I tried to call the inspector. It didn't go through, the lack of bars on my cell phone explaining why. Surely the area closer to Dornoch would have coverage. I'd try again in a few minutes.

The road followed the coastline, one I remembered as a beautiful drive, but hardly noticed today. Dolphins and seals played in the firth when Vicki and I made the trip. The seaside resort once was a royal burgh and is known for pebbles along the beach that are the size of a man's fist. Dornoch means pebbly place. Dornoch also had gone down in infamy as the last place in the Highlands to burn a witch—Janet Horne in 1727. We'd visited the Witch's Pool and the stone commemorating her death.

The GPS told me that I'd arrived at my destination.

I turned onto Beach Road and pulled over, deciding not to announce myself by driving up to the cottage.

I had limited coverage, enough to make a call, but the inspector didn't answer on his end. I assumed he himself had entered a low cell tower area. A sense of urgency covered me like a shroud.

I stepped out of the car, silenced my phone, tucking it into one pocket and placed the pepper spray into another. For the first time since becoming a voluntary constable, I wished I was investigating in the states where law enforcement officials are armed.

I began walking up the drive, leaving my car on the road. The cottage at number 124 was whitewashed. Bluebells and primrose burst from a small garden and evergreens lined the drive. The air smelled of pine resin. And a red Audi was parked next to the cottage.

Something wasn't right. This wasn't Morag's car.

"Are you sure about that address?" I stage whispered to Sean, turning back to the road, noting that I'd missed several calls from him as well as two from the inspector in a matter of minutes.

"142 Beach Road, like I said."

"You said 124. You inverted the numbers. Are you sure this time?"

"I'm sure. But ye need tae wait fer backup. The inspector's been trying tae reach ye. He discovered there was a Woodward sister. Mia Woodward. And she's an unstable one at that. Been in and out o' treatment centers."

Could news get any worse? The inspector wasn't close enough. Another hour or more and anything could happen to Rhona. "Did he see a photograph? Anything to connect her to Morag?"

"No such luck."

"How long before you can get here?" I asked.

"I don't have me beat car. Vicki's broke down and she borrowed it fer shopping in Inverness."

Apparently, the news could get worse.

"How could you do that?" I hissed. "Of all the…thanks for nothing."

And I hung up.

Calm down. Take deep breaths. You don't know for sure that Morag has Rhona. Or that she's the mentally disturbed sister of the dead patient.

I found the situation more distressing than ever. The least I could do is find out if Rhona was in the cottage. Then I'd make a decision whether to wait over an hour for the inspector or risk a confrontation on my own.

Morag's Vauxhall Corsa was parked in the drive. The cottage needed a fresh coat of paint and the flower beds were overrun with weeds. Nothing at all like the house next door. But, like the other home it had access in the rear to the coast.

Should I peek in the windows? That might expose me and my intentions. I couldn't see a way around it.

I marched up to the cottage and knocked.

The door swung open as though I'd been expected.

Chapter 22

Morag had her car keys in her hand and was obviously in the act of departing. Her poker face told me nothing, whether she was surprised at my arrival or not.

"What are you doing here?" she asked, voice neutral, not pleasant, but not cold either.

I'd rehearsed on the drive and acted as believable as possible. "Your vehicle registration is linked to this cottage. I'm glad I found you. Rhona has a family emergency, but her daughter can't find her. I was hoping she was with you."

Morag studied me, and I buried my liar's face under a look of deep concern that wasn't so hard to achieve considering present company. "She's here, down by the water, collecting pebbles fer her collection. I'll show you where."

"I really need to—" I hesitated, taking a step forward. "Would you mind if I used your bathroom first?"

What could she say? I'd taken another step forward and she'd taken one back, allowing me enough of an advantage.

She tucked her car keys into the light windbreaker she wore, stepped aside, and let me pass.

My intention was to slow us down to give the inspector time to get to the cottage so I wouldn't have to handle her alone. Although, was what Morag claimed true? Was Rhona collecting rocks?

In the bathroom, I did what every good television investigator would do. I waited an appropriate period of time before flushing the toilet to mask the sound of the medicine cabinet opening. Next, with water running, I scanned inside drawers in a chest against the opposite wall.

I almost missed it, but not quite. Under a stack of white bath towels, I found a red purse.

I'd seen it on the bar counter. It belonged to Rhona.

My heart jumped into my throat. After all my theorizing and with all my imaginings, I hadn't anticipated a situation like this. Trapped alone with Morag. Rhona most likely dead. The killer on the other side of the door, playing cat and mouse with me.

And while I thought I'd been crafty with the bathroom ruse, I'd also given her plenty of opportunity to arm herself against me, if she hadn't been armed already. I palmed the pepper spray as I opened the door.

"Okay," I said, emerging. "I'm ready."

Morag led the way through a garden in the rear of the cottage, opened a gate, and walked onto weathered wooden steps leading down to the rugged coastline. She descended first, calming my fear that she would ask me to walk down ahead of her. At least I was safe from a rear attack until the bottom.

"The pebbles that she wanted are the larger ones down that way." She gestured to the left. "We'll most likely find her there with the bucket she brought along." Morag headed in the direction she'd indicated, discussing pebbles. "Flint, quartzite, granite, pumice. This is considered a shingle beach because of the pebbles."

"A rock collector's paradise," I said, stepping over a sea of small pebbles along the shore, balancing carefully as they were wet and slippery. Waves slapped sharply at my feet, the width of shoreline narrow between the sea on one side and steep cliffs on the other.

"This is as far as I'm going," I said, stopping after scanning the beach in both directions. "I don't see her."

"There's a cave not far, set into the cliff. Maybe she's inside."

"Why would she be inside a cave?"

Unless she's dead and the cave is her coffin. Was it to be mine as well? What had I been thinking to come down here alone with Morag?

She faced me, too far to hit her with pepper spray, a small gun drawn from her jacket. I'd done police homework regarding just such an event. Instead of carrying a deadly weapon, I was instructed to make eye contact, to talk and to attempt to humanize myself.

I never felt so helpless and exposed.

I also knew that gun fights in the movies weren't realistic. Accuracy only comes with practice. Did Morag have the skill to hit me? She'd have to take a stance and take time to aim through the sight.

"Talk to me," I said, making eye contact. "Where is Rhona?"

"Dead. She figured it out. Even before ye did yerself, giving me no choice."

I shook my head, not having to feign sadness, and took a step forward. "Your real name is Mia Woodward."

She nodded. "I changed it before I began searching for the doctor. The internet is a wonderful thing. It took some time, but my hard work paid off and I came for him." Her trigger finger had relaxed, the barrel of the gun still pointed in my direction, but the barrel now pointed down at rock level.

Keep talking. "You were checking out the surgery. I have the wig."

"Where is it?"

"In evidence," I lied, wishing it wasn't in my car. "You need to turn yourself in." I was on high alert, trying not to stare at the gun. Eye contact. Communicate.

Morag sneered. "He killed my brother and got away with it. My plan should have been perfect. I'd stab him tae death after the supper that yer friends so graciously invited me tae attend, then fake the robbery tae establish an alibi. But then that silly, vain man gave me a better idea, an alternate plan."

"You decided to murder Stuart and set up Teague."

"Yer too smart fer yer own good."

"I'm smart enough to make sure I have backup," I said, turning my head and raising my eyes to the top of the ridge as though expecting someone. I took another step toward her, the pepper spray slick in my sweaty palm.

"I don't believe a word ye say. Yer one of those do-gooders just like Rhona. And yer careless, bursting into bad situations on impulse." She smiled smugly after noting my discomfort at her true words. "I'm a gambler and can read ye like a deck of cards."

"How did you take Stuart's knife away from him and how did you know how to use it?"

"I appealed tae the pompous arse's ego, admiring his sgian-dubh, asking tae take a closer look at it, and he handed it over. And as tae the proper knowledge, ye can find anything on the internet. I studied anatomy lessons so I could use my new skill on the murdering doctor. Justice has been served and yer not about tae ruin it."

Morag grinned, her eyes for the first time showing the depths of her hatred, the insanity within her. "To the cave," she said. "You first. After you drop whatever is in your hand."

I stared into the barrel pointed directly at me.

I considered running into the waves, but the water wasn't deep here, so diving down to avoid a spray of gun fire wasn't a viable option. I'd be forced to move slowly over the stones and my exposed back would give her time to sight in on me.

Instead, I had no choice but to drop my only weapon.

"Get moving."

I passed close to her and pretended to slip on the wet pebbles. My arms shot out as though struggling for balance, while throwing my shoulder into the arm holding the gun. To my utter surprise, Morag went down flat on her back.

She struggled to sit up, to take aim.

But I was on her.

We wrestled for possession of the weapon. Both of our hands gripping it. Both of us panting with exertion. I felt all-consuming fear mixed with a growing sense of rage. This crazy woman had killed

Stuart and Rhona and was trying to gun me down. Adrenaline seemed to give me renewed strength.

I blindly found one of the large pebbles with my free hand, closed my fist around it, hauled my arm back, and struck Morag in the forehead with as much force as I could muster.

Her body relaxed momentarily, allowing me the opportunity to grab the gun from her and rise. At first her expression registered surprise. Then I saw her vision clear, her eyes narrowing. Morag rose on one knee, staring at me.

I struck her again, not holding back, not caring whether I seriously injured her or not. All I knew was that Morag had to be stopped.

She rolled back down. I pulled out the handcuffs I'd recently been approved to carry and restrained her with them.

Satisfied that she wasn't going anyplace soon, I demanded, "Where is Rhona's body?"

After a pause long enough that I seriously considered kicking her until she answered, she muttered, "In the boot."

Chapter 23

I pulled the keys out of her pocket and made
my way as quickly as I could through the pebbles.
They became smaller again on the cottage side of the
shingle beach. Taking the steps two at a time, the
gun dangling in my hand, I ran to Morag's car.

There I hesitated, not sure if I could bring
myself to open the trunk and witness whatever
gruesome act had been committed on Rhona. I
heard a car approaching and looked up to see the
inspector's police vehicle pull up with Jamieson
driving and Sean riding in the back on the driver's
side. Leith Cameron burst out of the passenger seat
and headed my way.

"Go through the garden and down the steps,"
I told the inspector, who was right behind him.

"You disarmed her?" the inspector asked,
veering my way, his eyes widening when he saw the
gun in my hand.

"She's cuffed. Here, take this thing."

Jamieson accepted the weapon and ran for the steps, calling to Leith, "I can handle a handcuffed woman on my own. Make sure Eden's all right."

Leith pulled me to him in an embrace. I'm pretty sure I clung to him like a lifeline that had been thrown to a woman drowning in sorrow. Tears threatened now that I felt safe.

But a banging sound from inside Jamieson's police vehicle ended the moment. Leith released me. "We left Stevens locked in the backseat," he said, walking over and opening the door.

"I'm going tae help the inspector," Sean called, hurrying away.

"What are you doing here?" I asked Leith.

"I called the station looking fer ye, since ye weren't answering my calls."

"I never got them."

"Stevens explained how ye were after a suspect and that the inspector was on his way. I hitched a ride with Jamieson, meeting him out on A9. I wanted tae talk tae ye about something important tae me, but it can wait until we handle this situation."

He took my hand in his. I looked at our locked fingers. At his hand, realizing it was the same tender hand from my reoccurring dream, that of the faceless lover.

"I need to talk to you too," I said, feeling an electric current charging through my body and allowing it to release instead of bottling it up.

Ami had been right all along. But I'd been too afraid to risk opening my heart, afraid that he wouldn't feel the same. But his eyes told me otherwise. Our friendship was about to become something much more. I knew it with total confidence.

But could the timing be any worse? "Rhona Selkirk's body is in Morag's trunk," I said.

"Let's open it together then."

Leith took the key from me, turned it in the lock, and I heard the latch release.

Watching with dread, my stomach lurched as he opened the trunk to reveal the inside.

Rhona's tiny body was lying on a sheet of black plastic, her hands tied behind her back, her mouth taped shut. And her eyes were open wide.

My fingers groped to find a pulse at her neck.

Then she blinked, not once but several times.

219

Relief flooded over me, I ripped off the tape covering her mouth.

"About time," she crabbed.

Chapter 24

Four of us gathered at the Kilt & Thistle, each with a pint of ale to celebrate the end of a difficult case. Vicki, Sean, Leith and myself. We'd added an additional chair to the table for the inspector's arrival, as he was running late.

"The doctor's name has been cleared," Vicki said. "But the story is out."

"I was afraid of that," I said. "He's ruined."

"Not necessarily," Sean offered. "He's planning tae do an interview with the newspaper, confront it head on. He says he'll let the villagers decide based on his work so far as their doctor. He's confident that this will pass."

"Good fer him," Leith added. "It might even be a relief fer him tae have it out in the open. Hiding a secret like that takes its toll."

He smiled at me and his blue eyes sparkled.

We'd had *the* talk and discovered that we'd both felt the same way about each other. But we'd built emotional shields to protect us from making the same mistakes as we'd made in the past. The two of us carried baggage that would have to be addressed.

However, just recently, Leith had conquered a raging storm that threatened his life, and I'd defeated a murderer in hand-to-hand combat. If we could accomplish those daring feats, we could overcome something as simple and easily diagnosed as commitment issues.

As Sir Walter Scott once said, *For success, attitude is equally as important as ability.*

And right now, I was full of attitude.

And besides, life really was good. Mia Woodward was behind bars, Andy would be serving jail time for his latest shenanigans, and the inspector had warned him to stay clear of Glenkillen once he's released. So, the village is free from both of them.

A familiar piano riff played from my cell phone, announcing a text from Ami. "A happy ending for you!!!"

"A happy beginning," I replied, smiling over at Vicki, who I was sure had been gossiping with Ami while I helped Jamieson book Mia Woodward. News travels fast.

I feel sorry for Mia Woodward," Vicki said. "A troubled teenager, a disturbed adult."

Sean nodded. "Her parents convinced her tae seek help after her brother died. She even did some time as an inpatient. It's clear that none o' it helped."

I didn't feel sorry for her. Maybe with time I could look back with more empathy, but the woman had tried to kill me. And she would have done the same to Rhona.

Speaking of the aging spitfire, I saw her bang into the pub with her big red purse and that blue-tinted hair. She marched over.

"When do I get my badge?" she said to Sean, hands on hips.

My mouth fell open.

Sean gave me an apologetic grimace. I gave him a dark questioning one.

"You were busy with…ye ken…the case and yer new boyfriend," he explained to me. "And the inspector approved another special constable tae help share yer duties, lighten yer load."

"My load is fine," I insisted.

"I took it upon meself tae offer Rhona the position. Trial period, o' course."

"It's Constable Selkirk tae you," Rhona told him. "And I need some weapons tae carry in my handbag."

That's not happening anytime soon, I thought.

"Well, what are ye doing sitting around on yer derriere," she said to me. "I'm here fer training."

Leith laughed. "Sit down, Constable, and join us in celebration."

"Celebration of what?"

"A long life fer all of us."

Rhona took the chair reserved for the inspector. "Now *that* is worth celebrating."

Leith squeezed my hand under the table.

Before long, the inspector joined us, nabbing another chair and placing it beside me, Leith on one side, the inspector on the other.

Jamieson winked at me and addressed Sean, "So when are ye going tae break in the new constable?"

"Me? Not hardly. Tis up tae Eden."

"I don't think so," the inspector said. "Ye recruited her, ye train her."

Sean glanced at Rhona. "As long as ye know who the boss is, that being me."

"We'll see," she shot back.

Officer Stevens and Constable Selkirk teaming up?

What could possibly go wrong?

Hannah Reed, (aka Deb Baker) is the national bestselling author of the Scottish Highlands Mysteries, including *Off Kilter*, *Hooked on Ewe*, and *Dressed to Kilt*. She is also the author of the Queen Bee Mysteries. Under her own name, Deb Baker pens a Yooper series. Deb's Scottish ancestors were seventeenth-century rabble-rousers who were eventually shipped to the new world, where they settled in the Michigan Upper Peninsula.

Made in the USA
Middletown, DE
04 December 2023

44079359R00135